Brat Princess

First published 2008 by Kingfisher

This edition published 2009 by Macmillan Children's Books
a division of Macmillan Publishers Limited
20 New Wharf Road, London N1 9RR
Basingstoke and Oxford
Associated companies throughout the world
www.panmacmillan.com

ISBN 978-0-330-51028-8

1 3 5 7 9 8 6 4 2

A CIP catalogue record for this book is available from the British Library.

Printed and Bound in the UK by CPI Mackays, Chatham ME5 8TD

Brat Princess

Zodiac Girls

Cathy Hopkins

MACMILLAN CHILDREN'S BOOKS

Chapter One

Welcome to my world

"No. I am not ready. Do I look like I'm ready?"

I was lying on a sun lounger by the pool at our villa in St Kitts in the Caribbean, my mobile in one hand, a chocolate milk-shake in the other. Coco was lying on the sunbed next to mine, also wearing shades. She's my dog – a pink bichon frisé. (Everyone at my last school had a dinky dog, but no one had had theirs dyed the way I had. I had to do something – all the pooches looked the same, white and cute but now Coco stands out in a crowd and matches my new nail colour *perfectly*.)

I'd just been thinking how utterly cool life was here on this paradise island when I was interrupted by a demand as to whether I was ready to leave. Anyone with half a brain should have been able to see that I was no way prepared to board a flight to Europe. Like what kind of idiot would travel to Paris in a turquoise bikini? Even if it is from Prada's new collection and on everyone's must-have list for the season? We used to live in England when I was younger so I know how cold it can get over in that part of the world. Like, Brrrfreezingville.

"Sorry, Miss Hedley-Dent, but…" whinged Henry. (He's my dad's chauffeur, PA and handyman, though you'd hardly know it. In his usual garb of Bermuda shorts and Hawaiian shirt, and with his shoulder-length blond hair, he looks more like a professional surfer than a servant.)

"What now, Henry?" I was beginning to feel cross and would have been more snappy if it weren't for the fact that my friend Tigsy was on hold, waiting for me, on the other end of the phone.

"Just, er… the plane has been ready for some time and the pilot has been waiting for you for over an hour."

"So? Tell him that he may have to wait *another* hour because I am not ready and I want to catch some more rays before I leave."

"May I at least give him some idea of when you may be ready for take off?"

I gave Henry my best withering look. Tigs and I'd practised it for ages in the mirror at school last year before I got expelled. One eyebrow up, nostrils breathed in and lips tight. Tigsy said that I appeared more constipated than cross when I did the "look" but, whatever, Henry got the message, backed out of the room and closed the door. He's so pathetic when he does that droning on thing. Like timetables... airports... Like it's my problem. Not.

At last I could resume my call. I lay back on the lounger, took a sip of my milk-shake and, *erg*hhh... I spat out the shake. It was *LUKE*WARM!

"Shirla. SHIRLA," I called.

A few minutes later, Shirla, our Caribbean housekeeper, came out from the house. She always does everything sooo slowly. Like it's all one mighty effort. Probably due to the fact that she is about five million stone heavy. She's like a house on legs. Legs that are made of jelly – she doesn't so much walk as wobble her way along. I pointed at the glass. "More ice. And a dab more of that yummy chocolate."

"Oo you likes the chocolate. If you not careful girl, you going to become one big melted chocolate in that sun," she said as she swayed over, took the glass, then waddled off towards the kitchen.

"Oh and can you get Mason to do me some chips before the flight takes off. Those big square ones he does. And bring a little pot of that scrummy sour cream and chives to dunk them in. And something for Coco." (Mason's our cook and Shirla's husband. They're an odd couple, he's as skinny as she is large.)

Shirla stopped for a moment. "Uhuh, I guess I could," she said, "but you ought to eat some greens one of these days or else them spots on your chin there are going to be breaking out all over your pretty little face. And don't you go giving that dog no chocolate neither. It ain't right." She tutted to herself then disappeared inside before I could say anything.

I picked up the phone again.

"Yum. Chips," said Tigsy at the other end. "Think I'll get our maid to do me some. I lurve chips."

"Sorry, Tigs, guess you heard all that? Like, welcome to my world. Can you believe it? Henry trying to tell *me* when we have to leave, like, who pays who round here?"

"*Exactement*," said Tigsy. "You have to let them know who's boss, yeah?"

"Yeah. It's Mummy's fault. She's way too nice with them all. Like a little mouse. She's like, er, pardon me for squeaking. And Dad's never here, so what can one expect? It's left to me to let them know who's in charge. Like I haven't got enough to do as it is."

"Totally."

I stared out over the infinity pool and the sea beyond. It was glistening with a thousand tiny stars in the afternoon sun. "Yeah. Like sometimes I think that just because I'm only fourteen, they, like, think they can tell me what to do. But I say, no way. No way."

"Yeah. No way. Er, but, Leonora, I'm not being difficult or anything but one thing I do know and that is that sometimes when travelling, like, doing a strop can work against you. Like, it's the beginning of December, coming up to Christmas yeah?"

"Yeah. Like, deck the halls with Christmas holly, blah de blah de blah, de blah de yawn."

"So everyone's on the move, yeah? Not just us?"

"I guess."

"Well, I know from when Daddy does his own bookings for coming into land in our ickle jet, if you miss your slot, particularly at busy times, you don't get another."

"Oh. Un problemo you think? So you're saying what exactly?"

Tigsy laughed at the other end of the phone. "That you'd better get your stonkingly rich butt off that island in the Caribbean, Leonora Hedley-Dent, and onto the jet or else we're not going to be able to do our shopping trip in Paris and get back in time for Christmas."

"Like I care about Christmas. Hah bumhug to all that, I say, it's just *another* excuse for the staff to skive off for the day," I said but I did get up, slip my feet into my Gucci mules with the kitten heels and make my way through the open French windows to my bedroom. Coco got up and followed me. She's sooooo cute. She walks like she's wearing heels too.

"I know," said Tigsy. "Three weeks to go and it will

all be one big bore as usual. The fun part will be you being here and the shopping beforehand, although there will be presents on the day. Daddy said he might get me a new diamond Cartier watch this year. I've put it on the list as I am getting tired of my Rolex. It's so last season. But really, Lee Lee, I mean, I'm going to be okay for getting to Paris. I'm in Geneva and only have to hop on a train to get there."

"It's cool. I get you. I'll get a move on," I said as I took a couple of chocolate bars out of a drawer and flung them into the suitcase on the bed. "I'm packing as we speak but I'm not going to let Henry think that I'm doing it for him."

"No. Course not. But do hurry. I've got no-one to plaaaay with over here."

"I'll see you soon."

"Excellent. Kissy-kissy. Daddy's booked us the whole of the top floor at the George the Fifth hotel. I've been there before when Imelda Parker Knowles had her sixteenth birthday bash there in the summer. It's utterly dinky. I think you'll like it."

"Sorreee. Packing. Be there. Bysie-bye."

"Bysie-bye."

I put my phone down by the bed and went to the mirror, spritzed on some of my Goddess perfume, picked up my brush and brushed my hair through. I was pleased with the way it was looking. The sun had made my new blonde highlights even lighter. One day, Shirla caught me before I'd used my hair straighteners. She said that I had fabulous hair. Hah! She has no idea of the work it takes to keep it looking good. Like, I would be mortified if anyone saw me with my hair in its natural state (curly wurly), but she said that it suited my birth sign, which is Leo. My hair, which is halfway down my back, is like a tawny lion's mane. *Huh. Like why exactly would I want to look like a lion, for heaven's sake?* I thought as I applied a slick of mascara. *Most of them have manky manes, hardly the honey and fudge organic highlights that Daniel Blake, stylist to the stars, runs through mine!*

I put in my blue contact lenses to cover my boring brown eyes, applied some concealer over my spots and glanced round to see what else needed to be done. Coco was watching my every move.

"Oh don't look at me like that, boo-boo," I said. "I'll only be gone a few days."

Coco rolled over on her back and wriggled on the bed. She's sooo sweet, even if her tummy is a different colour to the rest of her. (I ran out of dye.)

Mummy and Shirla had done most of my packing but I threw a few more things in, just in case. All essentials that they'd missed. Lip gloss. Latest chill-out CD. More choccie bars for emergencies. I glanced over at the photo in a silver frame by my bed. *Mustn't forget to pack that,* I thought. I never went anywhere without it.

It was of me and Poppy, my sister. It was taken when I was twelve and she was ten. Oh. Hair straighteners. I threw them in on top. I couldn't believe they'd forgotten them, although actually yeah, I could – another example of how nobody around here has a clue about what matters to me. To travel without them would be like being without an arm or a leg, they're that important. It was hard to know what else I'd need though. Tigsy said it was unseasonably warm in Europe, but it wouldn't be as hot as it was here on St Kitts. The only clothes that I'd worn for the past week were bikinis and sarongs. Still. If it got too cold, I could buy a new set of cashmere. I'd worn the ones I got last December at least three times in the winter season, so I was well due for new ones.

I pulled my fave pair of skinny jeans out of the cupboard and began to put them on. Erg. Arff. They were meant to be tight but not that tight!

"MUMMY!!!!"

Mummy appeared at the door a few seconds later. "Yes, darling?"

"My jeans! They've shrunk."

Mummy came in and watched me struggling to get the jeans done up.

"Er… you don't think, darling, that you could have maybe put on a teensy weensy bit of weight do you?"

I could feel a tantrum coming on. I could feel it in

the pit of my stomach bubbling and boiling like a volcano about to erupt, like, it was all right for her, she never put on an ounce of fat no matter what she ate. She was so lucky with her straight blonde hair and her perfect figure. She didn't look her age either, and people always thought we were sisters. As if. It soooo wasn't fair that I'd inherited Dad's frump genes and his stupid curly hair rather than hers. "Me? Put on weight! These are MY BEST JEANS. I HAD TO WAIT THREE MONTHS ON A LIST FOR THEM TO COME IN TO THE SHOP AND THAT DOPEY DORA OF A HOUSEKEEPER HAS GONE AND SHRUNK THEM IN THE WASH!"

For a split second, I swear I saw a hint of a smile cross Mummy's face which made me madder. She put her hand on my arm. "Now calm down," she said in a soft voice that made me want to hit something. "You're a growing girl…"

I brushed her hand away. "Calm DOWN? Growing GIRL? I CAN'T GROW ANY MORE. I'M *ENORMOUS AS IT IS*."

Mummy sighed. "You've got a lovely figure, Leonora, and fabulous long legs, you're—"

"WHAT DO YOU KNOW? I'M ALREADY A SIZE TEN AND EVERYONE IN MY CLASS IS A SIX OR A FOUR! And Lottie James is even a size ZERO! I'M AN ELEPHANT! MY WHOLE DAY

HAS BEEN RUINED. I HATE YOU. YOU NEVER UNDERSTAND."

I wriggled out of the jeans. They wouldn't do up no matter how much I yanked at the zip. I tossed them onto the bed then threw myself, front down, on after them. And then I went for it.

"WaaaaaaARRRRGGHHHHHHHHHHHHHH HHHHHHHHHHHHHH."

I thrashed my arms, pummelled my pillows and threw my legs up and down. And then I felt sick. Yes, I was going to be sick. I could feel it. I sat up. "And now I FEEL SICK."

Mummy looked at me with wide eyes and an expression of terror. *Why oh why couldn't she ever say or do the right thing when I feel like this?* I wondered. *I'm sure I'm adopted. I can't be her daughter. We're nothing like each other and she hasn't got a clue what to do with me.* My head started to throb. "And now I've got a headache coming," I wailed. "And I'm fat. And spotty. And it's all your FAULT!"

At that moment, there was a gentle knock at the door and Henry put his head round. I picked up a pillow and threw it at him.

"GET OUT! GET OUT. ALL OF YOU. OUT. *OUT.* I HATE YOU ALL."

Henry disappeared mega fast and Mummy scurried out like a frightened rabbit.

"WahurggghhhhhhhhhHHHH," I yelled at the ceiling. "*No-one* understands me. Not *anyone*. I *hate* everyone. I hate them all. I hate my life. I'm so ugly. And *fat*. I am soooooooooooooo unhappy."

Chapter Two

Rules for life

Rule one: I am going to go on a diet. A serious diet. In fact, I shan't eat anything until I am a size zero like Lottie. Or… Hmm… Maybe there's some miracle fat-diluter pill that Mummy could get me. Yes. Must be. Or maybe liposuction? Cassidy Poole at my last school had her bum done over the Easter hols. She couldn't sit down for weeks when she came back after the break. So maybe not that option. I so don't do pain.

Rule two: no member of staff must look at me until I am size zero.

Rule three: Shirla mustn't use that perfume she wears. It smells of vanilla and cocoa, and that makes me want to EAT chocolate.

Rule four: Shirla must come with me to Europe as she is the only person I can stand to have around me at the moment (as long as she doesn't wear that perfume).

I was ready for my trip, sitting on the patio with Coco and waiting for the car to take me to the plane.

I was using the time to come up with some rules to make my life more bearable. Not that anyone cared apart from Coco, who adores me. They were all too busy with their own lives. Daddy hadn't even called this morning to say goodbye. Too busy busy making millions. Still I supposed someone had to. He works with banks and although he'd tried a few times to explain what he does, I still don't get it. It's something to do with markets and shares and money going up and down. Whatever. Who cares? We're loaded. That's what counts. I have my own savings account with hundreds of thousands in it.

Mummy had been busy with Shirla in the kitchen working out the menus for Christmas Day. She was having a bunch of boring neighbours over this year and came out onto the patio laden down with recipe books. I so wasn't interested – like, Christmas in the Caribbean? It's not quite right. There ought to be snow, but even in Europe it hadn't snowed at Christmas for years and years.

"All ready honey?"

I nodded curtly. I hadn't forgotten how unsympathetic she'd been about my weight gain and come to think of it, she hadn't asked me what *I* wanted for Christmas dinner like she usually did. Not that it mattered any more because I'd be having a lettuce leaf and boiled water with a slice of lemon. That was all that

Madison Peters had for a whole term at my last school, and she was as thin as a rake. Miserable cow she was but then so would I be if that's all I had for weeks on end. I was fast going off my diet idea. Thinking about my last school made me feel sad for a moment. It was the fifth school I had been expelled from in over two years and it was where I had met Tigsy. I would be sorry to have to start another school without her – that is if Mummy and Daddy can find me somewhere that hasn't blacklisted me. Whatever. I suppose I can always do home schooling. Loads of people do, although I've heard it said that home schoolers sometimes lack social skills on account of not having mixed with other people. I wouldn't like that to happen to me. Last thing I'd want is to be thought of as lacking social skills or being difficult. I can be firm and strong-minded, but never difficult. Not me.

"And thanks for asking what *I* want for Christmas dinner," I said to Mum.

"Oh, didn't I? Oh. I meant to. Are you sure I didn't? Hmm. Oh…" Mummy blustered on, obviously embarrassed by the fact that she'd forgotten to ask. I decided to put her out of her misery.

"Well, actually you needn't include me in *any* of the Christmas meals as I won't be having any."

She looked shocked. "Whatever do you mean, Leonora?"

"Diet. I am on one from now on. I shan't be eating again for at least a month."

Shirla came out behind her and overheard me. She was carrying my plate of chips. "Ah. So you won't be wanting these, then?" She dipped a big juicy one in sour cream and popped it into her mouth. I felt my mouth water as I watched her lick her lips. I do so like eating. It is one of my few pleasures in life. So sad that I will have to suffer and deny myself just so that I can look good in my jeans. Never was there a truer sentence than: you have to suffer to be beautiful. But... maybe I could start tomorrow. No. That would be awkward being in Paris and in such a swanky hotel. Shame to miss out. Best time to start properly is when I get back. Or in the New Year. Yeah. That's always a brilliant time to start with diets. Resolutions and all that.

"Er... Well. I ought to maybe just force something down before I go," I said. "And Mason did go to all that trouble of making them, Shirla." (Never let it be said that I don't appreciate what people do for me. I do.)

Shirla turned to go back inside. "No problem dahlin. Me likes the chips, too. Um, uh, they's good."

I made myself take a deep breath. "Shirla, give me that plate RIGHT now," I commanded. "And you'd better go and pack a case. I've decided that I want you to come with me to Europe."

Shirla stopped and looked questioningly at Mummy.

"But Henry is going with you. It's all been arranged," said Mummy.

"I don't care," I said. "I want Shirla. It's only for two days."

Shirla shook her head. "I's not going to Europe. Oh no, sugar. I's got things to do, Mrs Hedley-Dent. My little Mariah. She in the nativity play tomorrow night. She being a camel. I can't miss that, not for all the pea in China."

"Tea, Shirla," I said. "It's *tea* in China and anyway, there wasn't a camel in the nativity. There was a donkey though."

Shirla laughed. "Her costume got four legs that's all I know. And she sure look like a camel and I ain't missing her not for you, not for nobody. It's bad enough she didn't get the part she wanted, which was the Christmas angel, so I ain't missing it. No, siree."

Typical, I thought. *As usual, everyone is thinking about themselves.*

Mummy had her frightened-rabbit look on. "Yes, it's all been arranged," she said.

At that moment, there was a sound around the front of the villa and Mummy ran out to see who it was.

I turned to Shirla. "You *will* come with me," I said. "I can *make* you."

Shirla laughed, raised an eyebrow, did a perfect withering look and shook a finger at me. "Just you try,

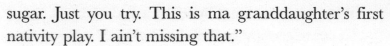

sugar. Just you try. This is ma granddaughter's first nativity play. I ain't missing that."

"Well *that* is your problem, Shirla. Don't make it mine. And by the way… I lent you a hundred dollars last week. I'm sure Mummy wouldn't like it if she knew about that! The staff borrowing money?"

"I ain't forgotten," said Shirla. She reached into the pocket of her apron and produced ten ten-dollar notes.

"Er… I don't think so. I want interest on it," I said. We did a class of economics at my last school. I knew all about lending and borrowing money. Our teacher had said that only a fool didn't ask for interest.

For a moment, Shirla looked as if she would have liked to throw the plate at me, but she held back and put her money back in her pocket. "Okay, missy, so how much interest you want then?"

"Five per cent."

Shirla shook her head and tutted then she handed the chips to me. "Uh-uh," she said as she turned and wobbled towards the kitchen. "Oo-ee. You sure is one precious madam. Uh-uh you is."

"And where's my princess?" boomed a voice from around the front.

Seconds later, Daddy appeared. I didn't even bother to look up, although I could see out of the corner of my eye that he had his smart work suit on, so he must have come from his office.

"What are you doing here?" I asked.

"Come to see my girl off," he said.

"But I'll be back in a couple of days," I said. "You've never come home to see me off before."

Mummy shot Daddy a "look" as if they'd been caught out. *They're up to something,* I thought. *Probably getting me some secret Chrissie present. Hope it's not another horse. If it is, I hope they get the right colour this time.* They got me a white one for my birthday and he had to go back because Mercedes Bernshaw had a white one and no way was I going to be accused of copying that loser.

"Come on, give your old dad a hug," said Dad and held out his arms.

I could hear that the car had arrived at *last,* so I got up and pushed past him. "Get real. I'm too old for hugs now," I said as he lost his balance and toppled into a flower bed.

An hour later, I was on the plane and on my way. *What a relief,* I thought, inhaling the comfortingly expensive scent of the leather upholstery as we took off into the sky. Mummy and Daddy had been acting really weirded out, like they'd taken lovey-dovey pills or something. Mummy was all clingy, more so than usual, like "Oh, my darling girl," and stroking my hair. Like, ew. I so don't do emotional. (Except with Coco. I was sad to leave her). It was particularly embarrassing with Mummy and Daddy because there was a tall handsome suntanned man with a mane of dark hair at the hangar who was watching me, as if he couldn't take his eyes off me. Okay, so he was way too old for boyfriend material, like, maybe old enough to be my dad even, but he had the X factor and probably recognized a kindred spirit in me, seeing as I also have it. I think he was a celebrity. He looked familiar – possibly an actor off the telly. It would have been something to brag about when I went back to school, that is if I'd had a school to be going back to. Or a bunch of friends to brag to in fact. I did once upon a time, but that was long ago. My sister Poppy and I had tons of friends and our house used to be always full of people, but I wasn't going to let myself think about then. It never did any good. I blinked back sudden tears and steeled myself. Past is past. Gone.

As the plane burst through the clouds though, I couldn't help but wonder what had come over Daddy. He was usually like me. Mr Unemotional. But even he had given me a big hug (when he had climbed out of the flower bed) as if he was going to miss me for once. Maybe they were both worried that the plane might crash or something. Whatever. I hadn't responded to either of their over-cringy goodbyes – like why should I pretend I was going to miss them? They didn't really care about me. If they did, they would have forced

Shirla to come with me. A small request, that's all I'd made. I liked Shirla. She's so totally a non-bull type of person and I had to respect that, though I didn't let on about it to her. *But no point in moping over it*, I decided as I put all thoughts of St Kitts out of my head. I looked out the window. Despite the bad start the day had got off to, I couldn't help feeling excited. Tigsy was good fun. Okay, so she wasn't Poppy, but we were going to have a top time in Paris.

To pass the flight time, I totted up my accounts and worked out who owed me what.

Shirla: $100

Henry: $250

Mason: $200

Plus interest at five per cent. I worked it out on my little calculator. It's a dinky pink one. Designer, of course. So cute. Cost a fortune. To get five per cent, you multiply by point-oh-five. Cool. And if they don't pay me back by January, I shall put the interest up another per cent. *Mummy and Daddy would be so pleased that my education wasn't totally wasted*, I thought as I tucked my notebook away.

There were still hours to go, so I read a few mags, watched a DVD, snoozed a little and ate a few of the assorted canapés that had been prepared by Mason before we left. I had to send a couple of things back – like when will they get that I don't eat avocados? I so don't do slime. I've told Henry again and again. As a punishment for him accompanying me instead of Shirla, I made him give me a manicure. When he'd finished, I told him I hated the colour and redid my nails myself. After that, I watched another movie, then dozed off again and woke to feel my ears pop. *Ah. We must be starting to land,* I thought as I took a peek outside the window. I'd been to Paris before and one of my favourite parts was seeing it come into view from the plane.

"Fasten your seat belts as we shall be landing shortly," came Pete the pilot's voice over the intercom.

We were still above the clouds so there was nothing to see as the plane continued its descent, but I kept looking and at last, we burst through clouds and I could see the ground below. *Erk? Fields and fields of green. What's that all about? Where's the Eiffel Tower? We must be coming in from a different angle to my previous trips,* I thought as I felt the wheels beneath the plane come out ready for landing. *I never realized Paris had so much countryside around it.*

"Plane ready for landing. Staff, take your seats," came Pete's voice.

Henry came in from the kitchen area, took his seat on the opposite side of the compartment and strapped himself in. I continued looking out the window. "Hey, Henry. Have we been diverted to another airport outside Paris?"

Henry looked down at the floor.

"Henry?"

He looked as if he was having an eye nerve attack and didn't know where to look. His eyes rotated round from his shoes to the overhead racks to the window. Up, down, around, but he wouldn't meet my eyes.

"Well?" I asked again.

"Um. Yes. Slight diversion I think. Slight. Yes…"

"You think? But why? Why didn't anyone tell me?"

"Sleeping," squeaked Henry. "You were sleeping."

"Don't worry, Henry. I'm not going to be cross, just I like to be kept informed. Is there bad weather? Fog? What is it? Snow?"

Henry was looking really peculiar. "Um. No. Temperatures are cold but no, no snow."

Maybe he's a bad flyer, I thought, *but… we've flown together before and he's never acted like this.* "Are you okay, Henry?"

"Oh yes," said Henry looking anything but okay.

I looked out the window again and got a strange feeling that we weren't over France at all. The fields below looked remarkably like… like England! I knew it well seeing as three of my schools had been there. A feeling of panic hit my stomach. *There was something going on that Henry wasn't telling me about. Oh god, the plane was going down. Must be engine trouble. Why else would we be landing here? Oh god, that's why Henry looks freaked. He knows. Are we going to make it? Oh god. I'm too young to die.*

I gripped onto the sides of my seat. "Tell me, Henry, tell me the truth. We're going to crash, aren't we? How bad is it?"

Henry kept staring ahead. He still wouldn't even look at me. *Must be really bad,* I thought.

"HENRY. *ANSWER ME.*"

I was beginning to feel really scared by now and felt a tantrum coming on. I hit the pause button on it. *Not the time,* I thought as I looked out the window again. We were coming in to land at a small airport. Definitely not Charles de Gaulle. *Ah, non, définitement, non.* I had been there. And this wasn't it. Not by a million miles. This looked more like a private airport. *Where were we?*

As the plane landed with a soft bump on the runway, the brakes screamed on slowing us down, then we began to cruise towards a hangar and small prefab building. *Not crashed then,* I thought. *Or maybe just one engine was in trouble and we had to make an early landing and Henry didn't want to scare me. That was okay.* I made myself take a deep breath.

"I'm okay, Henry. Now. All I need to know is what is going on. That's not too much to ask now, is it?"

Henry shook his head, unclasped his belt, stood up and began to walk past me. "Sorry," he mouthed as he disappeared out of the cabin.

Sorry? Sorry? What for? My mind went into overdrive. I quickly pulled my phone out and switched it on ready to call Tigsy, then Mummy. Before I could punch in Tigsy's number, the cabin door opened and the celebrity man who had been staring at me back in St Kitts was standing there. *How did he get on board?* I wondered as he beamed a kilowatt smile, revealing a set of Hollywood-white teeth. Then the penny dropped. *Ah! Hijacked. That's what's happened and Henry's in on it. I never trusted him. Probably in it for money. Happens all the time. He was always borrowing money and he could never pay it back. Oh god, how utterly dreary.*

"You won't be needing that where you're going, miss," said the strange man as he strode over to me, reached down and took my phone. "Now, if you'd like to get up and come with me."

Chapter Three

Pas Paris

"Who are you?"

Silence.

"Where are you taking me?"

Silence.

We were whizzed through customs and I found myself in the back of a car. A car with tinted windows so I could see out but no-one could see in. Celebrity man was in the front, and between us was a glass partition, but I could see that there was a gap in it through which he could hear me. There was no doubt about it, I had been kidnapped. I had done my best to resist getting off the plane but the man had simply picked me up, put me over his shoulder and carried me out to the car as if I were as light as a feather. Of course, I kicked and thumped but it seemed to have no effect at all. The man was a monster. Or wearing body armour. Whichever, his broad shoulders didn't seem to feel my protests.

"Can I have my phone back?"

Silence.

"I need to use the bathroom."

Silence.

"Look, my parents are very rich, but I expect you know that already. They will pay you off, no doubt about it. I even have my own account with thousands in it so how about we don't waste any more time, you let me speak to them, we'll get your money sorted and I can be on my way to Paris to meet my friend?"

More silence.

"Where's Henry? I suppose he put you up to this?"

Still no reply. I felt a tantrum coming on. "WeeeraaaarrrgHHHHHHHHHHHHHHHHHHHH-HHHHHHHHHH!" I blasted out. I pummelled the seats. Kicked the back of the front seats. Thrashed about. The man didn't take any notice at all. Not one bit. He didn't even turn around. *Hmm. Tantrum tactic not working*, I thought. *Best save my energy for later.*

I leant forwards to tap on the glass partition. And that was when I saw that he was listening to an iPod. No *wonder* he wasn't responding.

"Oi, dingbat brain," I yelled, but he was warbling along with some tune, totally oblivious to me in the back. I knocked on the partition again. Nothing.

I had no choice but to sit back and look out the window. It was beginning to grow dark outside, but I could see that the area was rural. We drove through a village with shops and where houses looked warm and cosy as people switched lights on and through one window, I glimpsed a family gathering round a fire. I saw a sign for the village as we left it behind. Osbury? *Osbury, sounds vaguely familiar,* I thought and made a mental note of it so that I could tell my rescuers later. After the village, the road grew dark again and we made our way through hedgerows, narrow lanes. *We are totally out in the country,* I thought as we sped along. *I wonder where X-factor man is taking me.*

After a further fifteen minutes, there was some movement in the front. I leant forwards to see that the driver had taken off his headphones.

"Hey," I said.

"Hey," he replied.

"Did you hear any of what I was saying before?"

"A bit. Who? Why? Where? Yeah. Heard all that. That's why I put on my headphones. Henry's on his way back to St Kitts. He had nothing to do with this."

"So who are you?"

"Name's Sonny Olympus."

I burst out laughing. "Sonny Olympus! What kind of stupid name is that?"

Sonny looked put out. "My name!" he replied, then he pouted like a spoilt sulky teenager. "And it is so *not* stupid. If you've really got a problem, though, you can call me Mr O, but only if you *must.*"

I laughed again. My tactic was to make him feel inferior. It works on most people. "Mr O! Pff. Also a stupid name. So who are you anyway?"

He turned and said proudly. "I am, or will be, like a ray of sunshine in your life. I am to be your guardian for a month."

"Oh, get a life," I said. "I'm a bit old for guardians wouldn't you say?" But something he had said had panicked me. A month. Whoever was behind this, Mr O or a whole bunch of them, they planned to keep me for a *month*. No *way*. Outside the scenery looked bleak, like we were driving through the moors. I felt a trickle of fear and, as a hundred horror stories began to play through my mind, I tried not to imagine what could happen to me in such a remote place.

"You did hear that my parents are very rich...?" I began.

"Yep, heard that bit. And you've got thousands. Lucky old you."

"So as soon as you call Mummy and Daddy, they'll pay."

For some reason, Mr O seemed to think that I had said something hysterical and guffawed loudly.

"WHY are you laughing?"

"Oh, I think you'll find that they've paid already," he said in a really girlie spiteful way. *Just who is this guy?* I wondered.

"Paid already? What do you mean?"

"Board and lodging. Hey, relax, kid. You'll see soon enough."

"Don't call me 'kid'. And relax? Are you from *another* planet?"

This caused Mr O to laugh more than ever. "Yes. Yes. Indeed I am," he said. "How *observant* of you."

Rude, sulky and sarcastic, and all in under an hour, I thought. *Boy! This guy could almost outdo me!*

He was starting to *really* annoy me. *Time to try another tactic,* I decided. I leant forwards and caught his eyes in the driver's mirror. He smiled. I smiled back. "You really are very handsome you know..." I began. Flattery usually gets you everywhere, particularly with boys, and although Mr O was clearly a man, what are men except older boys?

Mr O nodded his head. "Yes. I do know. People tell me all the time."

D'er. Modest, too. Not, I thought as I flicked my hair and did my best seductive look. Mr O flicked his hair at exactly the same time. "I'm sure they do," I said. "Now, Mr O, if you are nice to me, I'll be nice to you and..."

"Oh, for heaven's sake, cut it out. Who do you think you are? Lolita the teenage seductress? I'm way too old for you. *Way* too old."

"Okay, so how old are you, then?"

Mr O snorted. "Couple of thousand centuries. You?"

"Fourteen."

"Exactly. I rest my case."

"Anyway, that's stupid. You can't be a couple of centuries old. That's not possible."

"There are more things in heaven and earth than are dreamt of in your philosophy, kid," said Mr O.

"Oh, yeah? Says who? And *don't* call me 'kid'."

"Pal of mine name of William Shakespeare."

Oh, good heavens, I thought. *He thinks he's centuries old and a friend of Shakespeare's. He's a nutter.*

"I have my own money, you know Mr O…" I began again.

"I know. You said. Lesson number one. Money can't buy you everything and you'd better believe me, it won't where we're going," he said as we rounded a corner and I glimpsed the lights of a building ahead. It was hard to see in the dark, but it looked like an old fortress on top of a hill. The lights were on and cast a warm glow out into the dark night. *Our hotel,* I thought as Mr O drove up and stopped the car. *At least it appears that they're going to hide me somewhere decent.*

"I can walk," I said when Mr O opened the back of the car. "Just get my baggage will you?"

Mr O laughed and mimicked me, saying, "Get my baggage will you?" in a girlie manner as he held the door open for me. He indicated the porch at the front of the lodge as if to say that I should go in there. I took a quick look around to see if I could escape. The pale crescent moon behind the silhouettes of trees gave little light, but I could just make out gardens all around, although the shrubbery was dense black. I decided that I'd have a better look in the morning and make a dash for it when I had a better idea of where I was.

Mr O followed me up to the porch, *without* bringing in my bag I noted. The door was opened by a tall, black, fit-looking man with a shaved head and a chiselled jaw line. In the combat gear he was wearing, he had the appearance of a soldier, and like Mr O, he was incredibly handsome. Buff, as Tigsy would say.

As soon as we got inside the wood-panelled reception area and the man had closed the door, I ran over and hid behind him. I didn't like where I was. The whole building looked shabby and smelt of mould and mushrooms. On a battered table in a corner was a pot plant with half of its leaves dried up through lack of care. This wasn't a place I wanted to stay in for a moment longer than necessary.

"Quick, get the police," I said as I pointed at Mr O. "That man has kidnapped me."

"Is that right?" chuckled the man in combat gear. I nodded.

Mr O rolled his eyes as if he was exasperated, then

he examined his nails as if he was bored with me. "Now why would you think that?" he asked.

"D'er? I'm in a strange country, brought here in a strange car by a *stranger*. You do the maths."

"You haven't been kidnapped, Leonora," said the new man.

"How do you know my name? Oh *no*. You're in on it too. Who are you then?"

"My name is Mario. I shall be running the programme."

"Programme?! *What* programme?"

Mario turned to Mr O. "You haven't told her yet then?"

Mr O shook his head.

"No. He hasn't told me anything. What kind of hotel is this exactly?"

Mario laughed. "Hotel? *Hotel?*" He held his arms up to indicate our surroundings. "This isn't a hotel. Least not any longer. Oh no. Those days are long over. Now it's a boot camp."

"A *boot* camp?"

Mr O and Mario nodded.

I felt an awful sinking feeling in my stomach. "And why am I here exactly?" I asked although I was beginning to get the picture.

And it wasn't looking good.

Chapter Four

Queen of Sheba

"Look, let's get this sorted, then we can all be on our way. Let me speak to my mother. Um. Please."

Mario and Mr O exchanged looks.

"You told her the real news yet?" asked Mario.

Mr O shook his head.

"*Real* news? What are you on about?"

"Later," said Mr O. "All in good time."

"Two calls," said Mario, and handed me a portable phone from a hatch in the wall through which I glimpsed a drab-looking office full of files and cardboard boxes.

I took the phone and walked over to the corner. I had a bad feeling about what was happening and was totally unsure how to play it. These guys might be über good-looking, but they also looked as if they meant business. And they might think that calling it boot camp was some kind of funny joke, but I knew what was going on. I'd been kidnapped. I needed Mummy to get me out and fast. I dialled her number and she picked up straight away as if she'd been standing by the phone.

"Is that you Leon—?"

"Mummy, thank God. Shut up and listen. You have to act quickly as I don't know how long I've got but I've been kidnapped. I'm not sure where they've brought me but I'm pretty sure that it's England somewhere as all road signs and billboard posters are in English. I'm near a village called Osbury. Wasn't that near where we used to live when I was little? It looked familiar. Anyway, check it out and trace this call. Get the police on it and get them on it *fast*. I don't like it here. It's spooky and I don't know what these men have got planned. There are two of them so far, but there may be others."

There was silence at the other end of the phone.

"Mummy?"

"Yes. Yes, darling, I'm here…" She sounded as if she'd been crying. *So the dirty rotten scoundrels have been in touch already*, I thought. *Probably demanding their ransom.* Still. I didn't know why she was crying. We could surely afford it whatever it was.

There was a commotion at the other end and Daddy came on.

"Leonora?"

'Yes. Daddy. Did you hear? I've been kidnapped. Two men—"

"No, Leonora."

"What do you mean, 'no'?"

"No, darling. We… that is… your mother and I have paid for you to attend a… well… a sort of programme over there."

"WHAT?" I cried, causing Mario and Mr O to look over. "A programme? That's what they said. What sort of programme? Noooooooo. I don't want to do a programme. I want to go to Paris with…"

"Boot camp," Daddy interrupted and this time his voice sounded firm. "We've had enough of your behaviour, Leonora. You left us no other option."

A quick replay of their emotional goodbye flashed through my mind. Mum not asking what I wanted for Christmas dinner. Both of them acting guilty and clingy. Suddenly it all made sense. They had set me up!

No WAAAAAAAAAAAAAAAAAAAAAAAAAAAAAY! cried a voice in my head. "Daddy, I am sooooo *not* staying here. I *won't*. Get me out or send someone to come and get me and make it SNAPPY."

"It's only for a month," said Daddy.

"No. No. *NOOOO*. What part of that don't you understand?"

"A month, Leonora," Daddy repeated.

"A month? A *month*? Are you out of your mind? It's CHRISTMAS in three weeks' time! You can't leave me here over Christmas. I… you… they…"

"Goodbye, Leonora. They'll keep us informed of how you are. And I think you're allowed a letter once a week."

And then he hung up. My own father. Hung up. On me. I couldn't believe it! How DAAAAAAAARE he? I threw down the phone and kicked the wall.

Mario shot me a look as if to say, "Don't do that". *I wouldn't like to get on the bad side of him,* I thought. *He looks tough and a half.*

Mr O was more sympathetic and held up a finger. "One more call," he said.

I scowled at them, picked up the phone from where it had rolled under an old dusty chair and dialled the only other number that I knew by heart. Tigsy's. She'd get her father to rescue me. He was one of the richest men in Europe. Even richer than my dad. He'd sort it. And that would show the two losers standing behind me.

The phone rang and rang and rang. *Oh please pick up, Tigs,* I thought. *Please don't let it go onto voice mail.*

I was about to give up and try phoning Daddy back when she answered. "Hello. Tigsy Piggott's phone."

"Tigs, thank god, listen—"

"Hey Leonora. Where were you? Where *are* you? Daddy and I went out to get you, but were told the plane had been diverted. Then there was a message from your parents saying that plans had changed.

What's going on?"

I turned away from the reception area from where my two captors were still watching me. "Don't talk, listen," I whispered into the phone. "I've been... I'm in a..." For a second I wasn't sure what to say. I didn't want to admit that my *own* parents might have really sent me to boot camp. "I... I've been kidnapped."

Tigsy burst out laughing. "Oh, Lee-lee! You're such a scream. Kidnapped? Come on, where are you really?"

"That's just it. I don't know. In this place. It might be a hotel, but I think it might some kind of prison. It's cold and spooky, I don't like—"

"Oh you're *such* a drama queen when you don't like someplace," said Tigsy. "That's what you said about our dorm at school remember? But actually I feel the same about this place. People may say it's the best hotel in Paris and I know Daddy paid a fortune for us to stay here, but it looks like a prison to me, too. Like, I've only got four pillows and you know I like six. So when are you getting here? It will be so much more fun when you're here, too. We can play prisoners and escape together."

"No. Tigs. I'm serious!"

Suddenly the line went crackly.

"What was that? You're breaking up. Bad line. Can you hear me?"

"Tigs. I'm serious. Get help!"

"Can't hear you. I heard, I'm… I'm what?"

"Tigsy, get the call traced. Help!"

"Nope. Can't hear a thing. You've gone. Call me again in five."

"Noooooooooooooooooo… I don't get another call… Don't go."

"Laters."

And she hung up!

I turned round to face my captors. Mr O smiled and gave me the thumbs up. Mario looked at me as if I was a worm who had just crawled in from the garden. *Oh hell,* I thought. *I just landed in it.*

Best play along until I know exactly what I'm up against, I decided as Mr O gave me the guided tour of the lodge in his best TV presenter's manner, *then I'll plan my escape.*

"What is this building exactly?" I asked as we toured a maze of dingy corridors. They all looked the same – beige wallpaper on the walls, worn-out green-and-black tartan carpet on the floor and dim lighting from fittings on the ceiling that looked like they hadn't been dusted in a hundred years. I could see the bodies of dead flies and moths in the bowls of a couple of them. And the whole place had the lingering smell of boiled cabbage and lavender polish that reminded me of one of the boarding schools I'd been to. "And where are all the guests?"

"Guests? Hah! Oh, you'll meet them soon enough

although I wouldn't exactly call them guests."

"So what is this place, then?"

"Used to be a hotel with a fancy restaurant," said Mr O, "but as it's a bit out of the way, it wasn't doing any business."

"So what is it, then?" I asked again.

"Perfect location for a boot camp. The building was auctioned off in the summer and a few of us clubbed together and got it."

"Why is it the perfect location?" I asked, although I had pretty well worked out the answer.

"It's so out of the way," he replied, then laughed and said in a spooky voice. "No-one can hear you scream."

Play it very cool, I told myself as a shiver went down my spine, *very cool indeed.*

"Only joking," said Mr O. "No need to look so scared. Among other things, I'm an actor, you know." He smiled his kilowatt smile.

I scowled back at him. "I wouldn't give up the day job if I was you. You don't scare me with your silly scary voice."

"Well! You *are* a rude girl."

I shrugged. "So? Get over it. Maybe someone will take pity on you and give you a job as an extra in some movie that goes straight to video."

Mr O pursed his lips together. I knew I'd hit a nerve. *Hah. One to me,* I thought as he continued the tour and showed me a scruffy gym with some prehistoric-looking sports equipment, a dusty library that looked like it needed some books as most of the shelves were empty, a huge dark kitchen at the back of the building that stank of bleach and onions, and a dining room next to it with a long wooden table and benches in the middle. The whole place appeared shabby and uninhabited, which was what gave it the cold, spooky feel.

"That kitchen looks unused and it smells," I said as we made our way down yet another corridor.

"Yep. It's hardly been used since the place was a hotel, but that's all changed now. Hermie goes and gets what we need."

"Hermie? Who's Hermie?"

"He's in here," said Mr O as he opened a door at the end of one of the corridors. "This is the... er, the staff room."

It was like walking into a miniature planetarium. Gentle music tinkled from unseen speakers and it was warm with a lovely smell of baked apples and cinnamon in contrast to the rest of the lodge. A large mobile of the Earth and surrounding planets hung from a beam that ran along the centre of the ceiling. There were posters of the constellations and galaxies on the wall, and a painting of the signs of the zodiac. Four comfy-looking armchairs were placed around a roaring fire and sitting in the chairs were four people who were all staring at me. They seemed an odd-looking bunch. First was an old man with a tweed suit on and a white beard who looked like he belonged in a bygone age.

"Dr Cronus," said Mr O. "He'll be supervising your lessons."

"*Lessons?*" I asked as the bearded man gave me a curt nod. He didn't look friendly at all. "Like school?"

"Not exactly. More like karma," said Mr O. "You know – the theory that as you sow, so you shall reap. That's one of life's biggest lessons."

"Whatever," I said, and stifled a yawn.

Next to Dr Cronus was an extraordinary-looking woman who looked about thirty. She had long silver hair and the appearance of a mermaid without a tail. She had a dreamy expression in her pale eyes and was dressed in green and silver clothes that had an Indian hippie feel about them. *So last decade,* I thought as she glanced over and smiled at me.

"Selene Luna," continued Mr O. "She'll be your counsellor and nurse."

I nodded at her. *Yeah, right*, I told myself, *play along, play along, keep grinning. Don't let them know they've got me worried.*

The third person was Mario and I'd already met him. He didn't even glance up at me.

"You can call him War Bear," said Mr O. "And, if you like, you can call Selene Mother Moon."

"What's with the wacky names?" I asked.

Mr O beamed his smile. "It's what people do at boot camp. I've seen it on TV. All the organizers and directors have special names. Mine will be… er… let me think… er…"

"How about Dingbat Brain?"

Mr O actually considered it, then shook his head. "No. No. Not right. Instead you can call me… Sun Bird."

"Think I'll stick with Mr O, if you don't mind," I replied. "You might live in wacko city but I don't."

The fourth person was the most interesting-looking and for a brief second I forgot my fear. He was a boy babe straight out of a Calvin Klein commercial. Fit bod, great dark wavy hair to his shoulders and, like Mario and Mr O, the same handsome, chiselled features. I immediately felt more cheerful as I like boys, although this one looked at least nineteen, which is maybe a bit too old for me. He turned and gave me the same kilowatt smile as Mr O. *Must be family,* I thought. *There's something about them all that's similar – although I can't quite put my finger on it. Something in the eyes.*

"Welcome," he said.

"I shan't be staying," I replied.

"This is Hermie," said Mr O. "He's in charge of communications."

"And your name is? Big Bear? Small Bear? Furry

Bear?"

Hermie chuckled. "Hey, she's funny," he said to Mr O. "No. Although some people call me Mercury, you can call me Hermie here. I'll stick with that."

"No. You *have* to have a name," said Mr O. "Come on. Play the game. Pick a name. The rest of us have."

I glanced over at Mr O. For a moment there, he had sounded petulant. As if he didn't like not getting his way. *A bit like me*, I thought.

"Oh all right then," said Hermie. "I will be… Messenger Bear."

Mr O looked appeased. "Hmm. That's okay I suppose. You got her phone for her?"

Hermie nodded and reached into a desk behind him.

Phone? I asked myself. *These idiots were going to actually let me have a phone?*

Hermie tossed me a package wrapped in gold paper and everyone watched me unwrap it as if it was gift giving time at Christmas.

I ripped the last bit of paper. Inside *was* a phone and a small box. The phone was gold-coloured with a single and very large diamond at the top above the numbers. *Vulgar*, I thought. It didn't look cheap, but it wasn't exactly the height of sophistication either. The assorted nutters, however, were looking at me as though I'd just won the jackpot. *They really are mad*, I thought, *first they kidnap me, then they give me a phone, like d'er. Do they think I won't actually use it to phone for help?*

"You can use it to get in touch with me whenever you like," beamed Mr O.

"You? And why would I want to do that when you're right here in the same place as me?"

Mr O tapped the side of his nose. "Ah, but who knows what the next month holds? You might get lost when out on a hike. You might need to talk to someone. Oh yes, I think you'll find that you come to value that phone dearly."

"And I think that *you'll* find that, even if I did need to talk to someone, you'd be the last person on Earth. What makes you think that I would want to talk to you?"

"Because I am your guardian!" said Mr O.

I rolled my eyes. "Whatever," I sighed. I put the phone to one side and opened the box. Inside was a white gold chain with a charm on it. I looked more closely and saw that the charm was a tiny lion's head.

"The lion for a Leo," said Mr O. "Only very *special* people get these phones and a chain like that, and you have been chosen to join their ranks."

I tossed the phone and charm aside. "Yeah. Yeah. Whatever."

Mr O flushed red and looked like he was going to explode. I could see that a vein on his forehead was throbbing. "Well! You *ungrateful* little madam!"

Mario took Mr O aside and was talking to him as if trying to calm him down. *But what's the big deal?* I asked myself. At home, I have five mobiles and a whole drawer full of jewellery. No way was I impressed by these pathetic little trinkets that looked like they came out of a cheap Christmas cracker.

Mr O turned back into the room. "Hermie, give her the papers," he said.

Hermie reached into the desk, and this time he pulled out a sheaf of papers which he handed to me.

I glanced down. The first page had what looked like a geometric drawing on it. A circle with squares and lines all over it.

"It's your horoscope," said Mr O.

"So? Big deal. I already know my horoscope. Mummy has a private astrologer and he did my chart when I was a baby. He gives us updates every month."

"In that case you'll know you have some SEVERE lessons coming up, then," said Dr Cronus.

I stuck my tongue out at him.

He rolled his eyes up to the heavens. "Childish," he said, and Mr O nodded enthusiastically in agreement. "Might have known you'd respond like that. It's all in your chart. Childish. Spoilt. Stubborn. Used to having your own way. We need to put up some boundaries. Honestly. Leos. They all think that the world revolves around them. Always the same. And you're a Leo with

Leo rising and the moon in Gemini."

"So?"

"Moon in Gemini means that you have a short attention span," said Selene.

"And you're a double Leo. A right handful," said Mr O.

"And Mars in Taurus at the time of your birth, which can make you wilful and stubborn if you don't get your own way," said Mario with a shake of his head.

"Indeed. You've got a thing or two to learn all right," said Dr Cronus, then he seemed to lose interest and turned back to the fire. "Still. All in good time."

Mr O reached over and took the papers from my hand. "One thing that your astrologer *didn't* tell you and that is that, according to the stars, you are this month's Zodiac Girl. That's the real news!" At this point, all the people in the room nodded, albeit wearily in the doctor's case.

Mr O waited to see my reaction and I had a feeling that I was supposed to have fallen to the floor in amazement and kissed his feet. As it was, I was distinctly underwhelmed.

"Yeah? So?"

"I am saying that you are a Zodiac Girl," he repeated.

"Which means what exactly?"

"It means that, for one month, you get the help of me and my companions here."

"Like a special offer at the supermarket? Think I'll pass, thank you very much."

Dr Cronus tutted his disapproval loudly and Mr O looked very, *very* cross.

"Millions of girls would kill to be in your position," he said.

"Cool, so let them come here and be *Zodiac Girl* and let me go home or to Paris, which is where I'm meant to be."

All the gathered muttered more disapproval as I said this.

Mr O threw my horoscope in the air. "I am quite clearly wasting my time here!" He looked dangerously close to having a tantrum. "I don't think that you understand, Leonora," he said through gritted teeth. "To be chosen as a Zodiac Girl is a rare honour."

"Okay, so what do you get as Zodiac Girl? A crown? A sash? A certificate? There's only one thing I want right now and that is the fastest way possible out of here."

"You'll get a good caning if I have my way," said Dr Cronus.

"Yes. Whack her one," said Mr O as he made a fist and shook it at me. "She's asking for it."

Selene got up and came over to Mr O. "Now, now,"

she soothed. "That's not the attitude. She is a child."

"A child! No. I'm not. Go on," I goaded. "Whack me one. Come on, bite me. See if I care." I'd dealt with worse old codgers than him and Dr Cronus in my time. "But I have to warn you, if you lay one finger on me, I'll sue. My father has the best lawyers—"

"Zip it, zit girl," said Dr Cronus.

Zit girl! I put my hand up to my forehead where I'd covered up my spots that morning. My concealer must have worn off. "Buh… wuh…" I blustered. The old Crony had actually called me *zit* girl and now he was sniggering with Mr O as if they were ten-year-old boys who'd just made a really good joke. *How rude!*

Mr O composed himself then shook his head. "No, no, you're not getting it, Leonora. You have got the aid of the stars for one month. Don't you see how wonderful that is?"

I raised an eyebrow at him as if to say that, no, I didn't.

"It's true,' he said. "I am the Sun, Selene is the Moon, Hermie is Hermes otherwise known as Mercury, Dr Cronus is Saturn, Mario no less than Mars himself."

Oh. My. God. I'd been captured by a bunch of lunatics. I'd had enough. "Yeah yeah yeah. And I'm the Queen of Sheba," I said as I grabbed the zodiac phone and made a dash for the door.

Chapter Five

No escape

I ran down the maze of corridors not sure where I was going or what I was going to do. All I knew was that I had to get away. I ran through the empty kitchen and tried the back door. It was locked with three enormous brass bolts and no sign of a key, and I looked in all the nearby drawers, pots and jars.

I ran back through to the front and tried the door there. It was also locked. *Weird that no-one's coming after me,* I thought as I glanced down at the zodiac phone, punched in Tigsy's number and waited to hear it ring. Nothing. Maybe there was no signal in such a remote place. And then the phone rang. I pressed a button that was flashing green and listened.

"Hey kid," said Mr O's voice. "Just checking it's working."

"I can't call out on it. I just tried it."

"Oh, it's not for phoning out to anybody. Do you think we were born yesterday?" In the background I could hear laughter when he said this. "It's for you and me to keep in touch. I'm your zodiac guardian, remember?"

"Oh really. You and me?"

"Yeah."

"*Just* you and me?"

"And maybe the other planets that I introduced you to should you need."

I chose to ignore the "other planets" issue. "But I can't use it to phone out? Or receive calls from outside?"

"Nope."

"Oh really. Hmm. Well, I'll show you exactly what I think about that," I said and threw the phone down onto the floor, then stomped on it over and over until it was just a mass of splintered gold particles.

"You're going to regret that," said Mr O's voice from the splinters. "You have the Moon and Mars in your—"

I stomped on the phone again.

"Drama queen!" said his voice again. "Throwing tantrums is no way to get through life, you know. All I wanted to tell you was that it's a new moon tonight so things might get…"

And then it made a fizzing sound, a pop, then it went quiet.

Things might get what? I wondered as I ran back down the corridors and up onto the first floor which was deserted and where all the doors were locked with no sign of a fire escape anywhere. It was also strange that no-one had tried to follow me. I ran back downstairs and had stopped to catch my breath when the mermaid-looking lady came strolling towards me. She smiled then pointed to my right. "Down there and to the left."

And off she went.

What did she mean? What was down there? A way out? More lunatics who thought that they were planets? Supper? What? Thinking about supper made me realize I was hungry, *starving* in fact. *But where are the staff in this place?* I wondered. *The waitresses? And where's my suite? In fact, maybe I'll put off running away until the morning when I've had a good night's kip. If Mummy and Daddy have paid then the facilities are bound to be okay as we never stay anywhere less than five-star.*

I decided that I had nothing to lose by following Selene's directions and was about to set off when Hermie appeared. *Now who was he again?* I asked myself. *What had Mr O said? That Hermie was the delivery boy or the messenger or something.*

"Where's my suite?" I asked. "And I'd like a chocolate milk-shake and some French fries brought in. Mr O said you're the one who fetches what we need?"

Hermie cracked up laughing. "Suite? How should I know? I am Mercury. Planet of communication."

"So communicate. Tell me where my room is, then get me a milk-shake."

Hermie cracked up again and bowed. "Right. Chocolate milk-shake? French fries? I'll see what I can do."

"Thanks," I said. "And be quick about it."

"Sure. Quick is my speciality actually. I can be as quick as if I had winged feet sometimes," he said then winked. "In the meantime, you need to go down to the door on your left. It's time to sign in."

"You mean get my suite?"

Hermie nodded. "Yeah. To… get your suite."

I turned and made my way to the room he'd indicated. I opened the door and there was Selene behind a table with a pile of clothes on it. "How did you get in here?" I asked. I'd only just seen her a few moments ago, walking the other way.

She tapped the side of her nose. "The Moon has many mysteries, many secrets," she said, and she picked up a pile of clothes, a pair of trainers, a black baseball cap and a small brown paper bag from the table and handed them to me. "Now, first things first. You've missed dinner, so here's a sandwich, an apple and a carton of orange juice."

I took a peek in the bag and handed it back to Selene. "Er, no. I don't think so. I only eat red apples and that one is green. I don't eat brown bread, I only like ciabatta – toasted – and I don't do orange juice. I've already ordered some fries and a milk-shake."

Selene took the bag back. "Are you sure? You must be hungry."

"I'd rather eat my own arm than that."

"Suit yourself," said Selene. "You might well have to do that. But in the meantime, you have to change. When in boot camp, you have to dress like a boot camper. So, off with those clothes you've got on and pop these on."

I glanced at the clothes she'd given me. A navy fleece, trackie bottoms and a pair of plain white trainers. Off the scale of uncool. The trainers weren't even by a *cheap* designer. "Are you out of your mind?"

"So some folk say," she replied. 'I am the Mo—"

"Yeah, yeah. I heard Mr O's intro. You're the Moon. Good for you. And I'm a teapot. Yeah. We've been through the introductions. So. Where are my things and my suitcase?"

Selene looked taken aback. "In the vault. You can have it back at the end."

"End? But… you *can't* take my things away. They're mine."

She gave me a simpering smile. "Not any more," she said then held out a transparent plastic bag. "Now put your jewellery in here."

I put my hand up to my throat and fingered my

locket on its silver chain. A ripple of panic went through me. "No. *No.* I can't do that. I *won't* do that."

Selene smiled again. "We don't use the word 'won't' here. Nor 'can't'." In a second, her expression changed and became sad. "Now give over the jewellery." She held out her hand.

I wasn't actually wearing much jewellery, only my studs, my locket and chain and my silver bracelet. None of it was worth very much as I tend not to travel in my valuable stuff, but no way was I handing it over, especially not the locket. "No," I said. "You can take a hike." I noticed that she was wearing a necklace. It was a pendant with a circle in the middle and two half-moons on either side. "You've got your necklace on, so I'm going to keep mine."

Selene looked alarmed, like she was going to cry. "A hike at this time of night? No. Oh. Don't be difficult. I do so hate it when people don't co-operate. It can make me very *emotional!* And especially when there's a new moon in the sky like there is tonight. It's a time for new beginnings you know. A *good* time if you give it a chance and don't resist it. It can be a time for rejuvenation. So don't make me MAD! Lunatics, they're MAD aren't they? Lune. *Another* word for moon. Making sense now, is it? Moon. Lune. So I'm warning you, I can get *MAD.*"

I jumped back when she shouted the word mad as

she said it with such force. *Boy, Mr O said this lady was a counsellor, but she's clearly way unstable,* I thought as I made for the door.

"MARIO," Selene called and in an instant Mario appeared and blocked my way out. "Leonora doesn't want to hand over her jewellery."

Mario gave her a curt nod. "It's the rules," he said then he strode over and bent down so that we were nose to nose. "Now hand it over or else you and I are going to stand here all night."

I crossed my arms and shut my eyes. "Fine."

Seconds went by and I took a peep. He hadn't budged an inch. His big face loomed in front of me. We were almost eyeball to eyeball. At my last school, I could out-stare anyone but this guy was out of my league. I quickly shut my eyes again. *Out of sight, out of mind,* I thought.

Minutes went by and I took another peep. He hadn't budged.

"I'd give up now if I were you," Selene advised. "He can stay like that for decades."

"I am *not* going to give you my jewellery," I said.

"Yes you are, Missy. Everyone else does. Studs, piercings, bangles and beads. All in the bag."

"They're not worth anything. Honest. I have much more expensive jewellery at home and you're welcome to that just... *please,* don't make me take my locket off."

"And what's so special about the chain?" asked Selene.

I really didn't want to talk about it. I didn't talk to anyone about it. I didn't talk about any of my real feelings or fears. Not any more. I hadn't for a long time. "Nothing. Just I… I always wear it."

"And now it's time to hand it over," said Mario.

"No. Look," I said as I slipped off my bracelet and took out my studs. "You can have these. Come on. Meet me half way. I'm co-operating."

Mario took the jewellery I handed him and put it in the bag then looked back at me. "Now give me the locket," he said.

"*No.*" I felt a rising panic at the thought of being without it. "And you can't bully me."

"Not bullying you, missie. Just that's the rules. Now come on, what's so special about that chain?"

I pushed the feeling of panic away. Down deep inside. I wasn't going to let him know that I felt intimidated. I'd learnt that lesson long ago with Poppy. Never let them see how scared you are. "My sister gave it to me."

"And you'll get it back at the end of the programme. Now hand it over."

"No. No. NOOOOOOOOOOOOOOOOOOOO."
I lashed out at him with my arms and went to kick him, but he stepped back in the nick of time. Instead my foot

crashed into the wall.

"OWWWWWW! Oo-oo. OWWWWW. And now you've made me hurt myself. I HATE you. You're HORRIBLE," I yelled. *They could never understand about Poppy and me,* I thought. *Why should they?* "And I'm NOT getting changed into those clothes either. I mean, navy? HelLO? So last decade."

I wanted to throw an almighty strop, but got the feeling that I'd gone far enough and a mega tantrum wouldn't wash here. I also felt like I was going to cry. I started to shiver and Selene looked over at me with a sympathetic expression on her face. "Okay, look, Leonora," she said. "I'll cut you some slack seeing as this is your first night. You put the clothes on, you can keep the locket on. How about that?"

My first instinct was to tell her to shove it, but it was late. I wanted my chocolate milk-shake and fries. I wanted to go to bed and get some kip. I wanted these crazy people off my back. I nodded. "Okay. But ask him to leave."

"I'm away," said Mario. "No way I want to see your sorry butt in the buff."

And off he went.

"Good girl," said Selene as I picked up the clothes. She handed me a cup of what looked like water. "Now drink this water."

"Water? With nothing to flavour it?"

Selene nodded. "It's all you're getting."

"Okay but is it Peroni? That's the brand I drink."

Selene gave me a "Don't be so stupid" look. I took that as a no, so I took the cup and drank, but only because I was about to die of thirst or else I wouldn't have touched the stuff.

"Good girl," she said again.

I turned my back on her. She annoyed me. They *all* annoyed me. I wasn't a good girl. I knew I was bad. I took off my clothes and put on my prison outfit. I was exhausted, but tomorrow, *tomorrow*, she was going to see just how difficult I could be. And so were the rest of them. "Okay. So, please, can I go to my room now?"

"Sure," she said. "Follow me."

Chapter Six

The others

"No. This can't be right," I said as I looked around the dingy, narrow room that Selene took me to. With the windows so high on the walls that you'd need to stand on a chair to look out of them, it really did resemble a prison. Where was my private room? My bed? My luggage? All I could see was this unwelcoming dorm with three single beds on one side. No pictures. No flowers. No bowls of fruit or TV. No phone. No Peroni water. No *nothing*. Just beds, bare cream gloss walls and a couple of sets of drawers and a wardrobe. And it felt damp. I could see condensation on the windows and the glisten of moisture on the shiny wall just beneath.

Selene pointed at the bed that was furthest away on the right. "That's where you'll be sleeping."

"But... but it's not even made up!" I said as I took in the duvet, cover and sheet that were in a neat pile at the bottom of the bed. "And where are the pillows?"

"You have to earn those," said Selene.

"Wha...?!" I was so gobsmacked, I couldn't think of

anything to say. To think that MY mother and father had sent me here. I felt a rage inside the likes of which I'd never experienced before and was aware that my jaw had tightened, my fists clenched and I had a bitter taste at the back of my mouth. How DARE they? Even though I had no doubt that I'd be out tomorrow, to even leave me here for *one* night was unjust. *Bang* out of order. I was going to so make them suffer when I got home. In fact, I'd take them to court. I would sue them for unreasonable behaviour. I would sell my sad story to the tabloids to the highest bidder and that way I'd be financially free of them. Then I would leave home. Go and live with Tigsy. That would show them. No. Maybe not. They'd probably like that. Out of sight, out of mind. I don't think they really love me any more, so they'd be glad to get rid of me. I was a constant reminder of Poppy and what had happened, so they'd probably be happier if I went. So, no. I'd stay and make their life a misery.

"So, I'll leave you to it," said Selene. "You can make up your bed and then the others will be back soon from their hike and you can meet them after their supper."

I still couldn't speak. I pinched myself. Surely I'd fallen asleep on the plane and was having a nightmare? This *couldn't* be happening for real. I was Leonora Hedley-Dent. Daughter of Alex and Clara Hedley-Dent. We were loaded. We stayed in the kind of places that most people dreamt about. Places that featured in the top posh mega luxury seven-star locations on the planet. Not dingy dives in Loserville like this dump. So Mum and Dad didn't like me. So what? I still always got my own way. I did. I diiiiiid. Did. Did. Did. Did. Surely Mum and Dad couldn't hate me this much? I bent over, pulled at the bedding on the bed nearest and yanked it off.

"Er… Marilyn's not going to like that," said Selene.

"Never mind MariLYN. Who's she anyway? Actually, don't answer. I don't care. I've met enough deadbeat losers for one day. And you know what? LeoNORA doesn't LIKE IT!" I shouted, then proceeded to pull the covers off *all* the beds, shoved them on the floor, then stomped on them. Selene didn't attempt to stop me. In fact, she didn't seem bothered at all. She just waited until I'd stripped every bed bare then said, "Okay. Feel better now?"

"No I DON'T!" I yelled and made my way down to my bed, lay face down and thrashed away with my arms and legs.

As I wailed into the mattress, I heard the door open and close.

"Ah, a new girl," said a female voice.

"Yeah, and see what the stupid pillock has done to my bed," said a second voice in a Cockney accent.

Pillock, I thought. *Did someone just call ME a pillock?*

I stopped mid wail and tilted my head so I could see who had come in. Two girls were standing at the other end of the room staring at me. Both were medium height, one with dark, wavy, shoulder-length hair and glasses, the other with long blonde hair and a wide mouth. *Older than me,* I decided. *Maybe seventeen?* The blonde one was wearing a sleeveless T-shirt even though it was cold in the room and she had a tattoo on her upper right arm. *Tattoos are so has-been rock star,* I thought, *but I suppose she thinks that it makes her look hard.*

"Right, introductions," said Selene cheerfully. *She really is deranged,* I thought. *Like I'd ever want to meet these two?* "Now. This is Marilyn Brocklehurst and Lynn Bailey. Girls meet Leonora Hedley-Dent."

The dark-haired girl called Marilyn scowled at me. "'edley Bent is it? Oi, you, posh girl. You responsible for messing up my bed?"

Her friend sniggered and watched to see what I was going to do. I turned away.

"Oi, 'edley Bent," repeated Marilyn. "I wanna lie down."

I decided I was going to show them that they didn't intimidate me, so I sat up and looked over at them. "Then get one of the staff to do it," I said.

Lynn snorted with laughter and I saw Selene slink away and close the door behind her. *Oh God,* I thought. *She's left me alone with them.* Marilyn fixed her eyes on me, clenched her fists and approached. I took a sharp intake of breath and braced myself for a thumping. However, just as Marilyn got near, she slumped down on the bed next to mine.

"What you in for then?" she asked.

I felt torn. Part of me didn't want to talk to anyone. Another part wanted to know what was going on. Where I was. What the programme was all about. That part won. "Nothing. It's all been a huge mistake. I'll be out of here in the morning."

Both girls burst out laughing like I'd said the funniest thing ever, and Lynn came to sit next to Marilyn. "That's what we said too, when we got here," she said. "All a big mistake."

"Okay. So what you in for then?" I asked.

Marilyn narrowed her eyes and jutted her chin forward, "Murder. Din't like one of my teachers so I duffed 'im over one night down a back alley."

I cracked up laughing. "Yeah, right. Pull the other one. Do I look as if I was born yesterday?"

Marilyn looked put out. "Yeah, you do actually. And you'll gerrit too, if you don't watch it."

I laughed again, which I could see annoyed Marilyn even more, but I was sure that she was just trying to scare me and I was determined to show that I wasn't frightened in the least. "So what you really in for?"

"None of your business. You ask too many

63

questions," said Marilyn, who got up and slouched away.

"So what about you?" I asked Lynn.

"And what about you?" Marilyn mimicked in a posh voice from behind her. I ignored her.

"Yeah. Me too. Er… Murder," said Lynn.

I rolled my eyes. "Can't you think up your own dumb answer," I said.

"Okay, yeah. I'm in for drink."

"*Drink?*"

"Yeah. Cider. Baileys. Crème de menthe. I like to drink. Christmas liqueurs are my favourite but… I'm warning you, they have a funny effect sometimes. I don't know what I'm doing. They send me a bit…" she made a circle near her temple with her finger and made her eyes cross, "…demented. People say it's chemical like, but, whatever."

Behind her Marilyn chuckled.

"Yeah. Course," I said wearily as if I'd heard it all a million times. "Chemical. Whatever."

Marilyn began mimicking the way I spoke again. "Yeah. Course. Chemicaaaal," she said in her infuriating version of a posh accent.

"I do *not* speak like the queen," I said.

"Ay do not spake like the queen," she repeated.

I got up off the bed and moved away. Already I wished that I'd kept my zodiac phone. Okay, so I could only reach Mr O, but even he was better than these two psychos. Although I could tell that they weren't murderers and were putting on the hard act, I wasn't sure what the real story was and until I was, I thought it was best not to push them too far, especially as there were two of them against me.

"Yeah you do speak stuck-up," said Lynn. "Just remember, when we don't like someone, we do away with them so you'd better watch yer back, Smedley Pent."

I turned back to them. "Hedley-Dent," I said. "If you're going to say my name, say it correctly. And you don't scare me. So kill me. See if I care."

Marilyn raised an eyebrow, came back up the aisle and put her face very close to mine, not unlike the way Mario had before when I said I wouldn't take off my jewellery. Up close, she smelt of peppermints. This time, I didn't close my eyes and I made myself stare back at her. For a moment, my chest tightened as I thought she really was going to thump me this time, but she didn't.

"Later," she said then walked back up to the other end of the room.

Later what? Is she going to kill me in my sleep? I wondered as the door opened and two boys came in. One was dark, tall and lanky with round shoulders and a pinched expression on his face. The other, short one had red hair tied back in a ponytail and a friendly face. They surveyed the mess on the floor then looked accusingly at me. I did a half lip snarl back at them to show them that I was tough and not to be messed with.

"You're *not* telling me that we share with boys?" I asked.

Lynn shook her head. "No, they're in the dorm next door, thank God. Mark and Jake. Meet our new princess."

I gave them a royal wave to let them know that I wasn't intimidated by them either. The dark one shrugged and turned away while the red-haired one knelt on the floor and starting howling like a dog.

"Cut it out, Jake," said Marilyn. "No need to keep up the act in 'ere when it's just us."

This nightmare just gets worse and worse, I thought as I glanced over at Lynn and hoped for an explanation.

"Jake's playing the nutter card," she said.

"Nutter card?"

'Yeah, he's hoping that by acting insane, he might be sent home."

Good idea, Jake, I thought. *I should have thought of that.* I looked over at Mark, who had gone over to the window and was staring out into the black night.

"And Mark has taken a vow of silence," said Lynn. "Hasn't spoken for over a week now."

"A *week!* You guys have been here a week!"

Lynn nodded.

By the window, Mark had pulled a little notebook out of his pocket and was writing something. When he'd finished, he came over and held up the paper in front of me.

Keep out of my way and I'll keep out of yours. If not, you're dead.

"Oh, how sweet, another threat on my life," I gushed. "And sooooo nice to meet you too... loser." I stuck my tongue out at him. He scowled at me and went back to the window.

Selene popped her head round the door. "Lights out in five. Boys, back to your dorm," she said then disappeared again.

"But I haven't eaten anything and I'm HUNGRY," I yelled after her.

Selene's hand appeared around the door and dumped a paper bag onto the floor. It was the bag that contained the apple and the sandwich that she'd given me earlier.

"No WAAAAAAAAAAAAY," I yelled. "What part of NOOOOOO WAAAAY don't you understand?"

Mark, Jake, Lynn and Marilyn all seemed highly amused when the same arm appeared around the door, a little lower this time and took the bag back.

"Nollucks," said Marilyn. "I would 'ave 'ad that."

The boys left the dorm and, two minutes later, the lights did go out.

I sat in the dark for a moment and could hear Lynn and Marilyn getting into their beds.

"Er, girls…" I said. "Er… has anyone said anything about you being Zodiac Girls or anything about planets being here in physical form…?" I trailed off because it sounded insane.

"No. Why?" replied Lynn. "What you on about? You're mad you are."

"Oh nothing. Forget it," I said. *Maybe the planet nonsense is a special kind of torture they're saving just for me,* I thought as I groped my way to the bottom of the bed, grabbed the duvet and snuggled under it. I kept the horrible clothes on because I was freezing.

As I lay there and stared into the dark room, my mind played over the past couple of hours. It had been unreal. All that baloney about me being a Zodiac Girl? *What was that about?* I thought as my stomach growled. Mr O had kept saying that it was a rare honour. *Honestly! A rare honour to be put through this mortification and no supper either? If this is a rare honour, Mr O could shove it where the sun don't shine. This has to be the second-worst day of my whole life.*

I closed my eyes and tried to shut out the nightmare scenario. I was starving hungry and I'd never felt so lonely. I was also beginning to get the feeling that there wasn't going to be any room service bringing my chips and chocolate.

Chapter Seven

Wake up call

"Tan tah tat ta TAAAAAAAAAAAAAAAAAAAAAA."

It seemed as if I had only just closed my eyes when a *disgusting* noise blasted into the room. Like someone was playing a very LOUD trumpet a quarter of an inch away from my right ear. I came to with a jolt. I wasn't sure where I was. For one gorgeous second, I'd imagined that I was back in my room in St Kitts. Coco curled up on the end of my bed. Staff on hand outside to carry out my every whim. But no. It was dark in the room and I felt confused. It didn't smell like home. It smelt like… boiled onions and bleach with a trace of peppermint.

A light came on. An overhead *very* bright light. And all illusions were shattered as the previous day came back to me. I was in hell with a bunch of losers and our captors were psychos who thought that they were living embodiments of the planets.

"OhmigoooooooooOOOOOOOOOD," I groaned. "This caaaaaaaan't be haaaaaappeniiiiiiing."

"It can and it is, so zip it, posh girl," said Marilyn as she blinked sleepily in the next bed. "It's bad enough 'ere without you whining on."

Next to her, Lynn moaned. "I haaaate mornings," she said.

Marilyn stumbled out of bed with a scowl on her face. I looked at my watch and saw that it was five-thirty in the morning. I'd never in my life been up at that time in the morning! I snuggled further down into the bed. They'd have to drag me out if they wanted to get me up. For one thing, it was so cold in the room that I could *see* my own breath and, for another, now that I'd slept a bit, I felt my fighting spirit return and I had to plan out my course of action.

My fellow inmates fell out of their beds and out the door, which surprised me as neither of them had seemed like a pussycat the night before.

"Where are you going?" I called to Lynn.

"Bathroom then breakfast then chores."

"Hmm. Sounds like a fun day. NOOOOOOT. So. To get up and join you or not to get up? Hmm. What a difficult decision. Er… switch the light out when you go, Lynn, and ask one of the psychos to bring me a cup of tea in a couple of hours."

Lynn curtsied. "Why sure, Your Royal Highness," she said, "and I'll ask them to turn up the heating too should I?"

"Oh yeah. Would you? I'm amazed that we didn't all die of hypothermia in the night."

I turned over and, when she didn't turn off the light, I pulled the duvet further over my head. As I did, I noticed a note written on bright yellow paper flutter onto the floor. I picked it up and glanced at it.

Mars is in Capricorn at the moment and Saturn in Aquarius (that's Mario and Dr Cronus in case you weren't listening yesterday, Leonora). The day will start with an intense confrontation which you could learn from. Back down if you have any sense. And the Moon may bring up some painful memories. Remember what you resist, persists. Bye for now, kiss kiss, your guardian, Mr O (a.k.a. the Sun).

"The confrontation starts with you, saddo," I said as I ripped it up into little pieces. "And I'm not backing down."

A few minutes later, I heard footsteps and someone yanked the covers off. It was Mario. He was standing at the end of the bed, legs astride, hands on hips.

"Hey! Do you mind?" I said as I grabbed for the top of the duvet and tried to pull it back over me. "It's like a fridge in here."

Mario looked at his watch. "You got ten seconds, lady."

"Yeah, yeah, whatever," I said as I lay back down and turned away.

"Ten... nine... eight... seven... six... better get up,

missy… four…"

"Or else what?"

"No breakfast."

"Oo, so bite me," I said, but actually I felt torn because I was hungry. On the other hand, I didn't want to give in too easily.

"Three… two…"

I leapt up. "Okay, okay. Keep your hair on."

"Keep your hair on, *sir*. You will address me as 'sir' from now on."

"You have to be kidding. I have never called anyone 'sir' in my life and I'm not about to start now."

"I'm sure there'll be a lot of things you've never experienced before gonna happen here. Getting up at five-thirty for a start."

"Yeah, yeah. Sir. So what happened to Brother Sun, Sister Moon and all that rubbish?"

"That's for the others. I prefer you call me 'sir'."

"Oh, get a life, soldier boy. Now, tell me where to go for brekkie?"

A flash of annoyance crossed Mario's face and I saw him bite his cheek as if biting back what he'd really like to say. "I'll tell you where to go, but first you give me some respect, girl."

I did a jerky dance around the bed the way that I'd seen the cool rappers do on TV, then I put my forefinger and middle finger together and pointed at the floor, "Okay, my man, get down, get cool. Yo. Respect," I said in my best street-rapper accent.

Mario wasn't impressed. Or amused.

"You know who I am, girl?"

I nodded and did a mock salute. "The planet Mars. Here on Earth. In physical form, SIR!" And then I couldn't help but snigger. I mean, how utterly absurd! If Tigsy was here, we'd both be on the floor laughing our heads off.

Mario scowled. "According to your birth chart, I am here to teach you some respect for others Miss Hedley-Dent."

I began to do my rapper dance around him again. "Yo, get down..."

"Right, that's it," he said. "No breakfast."

I straightened up and stuck my bottom lip out. "Am I bothered?"

"You will be."

I stuck my tongue out at him.

"And that just earned you... no lunch either."

I stuck my tongue out at him again.

He turned to go and pointed at the door. "You'll learn. Bathroom out to the right."

After he'd left the room, I ran to the window to see if I could see where I was, but it was still dark outside.

I was bursting to go to the loo, so I went in search of

the bathroom. I didn't have far to go as I could hear the sound of water. And screaming.

"What's going on?" I asked when I opened a door and saw Marilyn by the sink.

She jutted her chin towards a door. "Shower. Cold. Lynn lost her 'ot shower privilege yesterday for giving cheek."

I couldn't believe what I was hearing. "You have to *earn* hot water?"

"You said it, princess."

"But that's inhumane."

"Innit? But try telling that to Mario," she replied.

Enough, I thought. *I don't care that it's still dark outside. It will be light soon enough.* I quickly used the loo, ran back to the dorm, put on my boot-camp trainers, grabbed the duvet and wrapped it around myself. It would help keep me warm when I was outside because I was leaving and *no-one* was going to stop me.

I tiptoed out into the corridor and crept out to the front. Miracle of miracles. The door was open!

I glanced behind me. No-one was about, so I opened the door and slipped out. It felt like I'd opened the door of a fridge, it was so cold out there and dark, and far away in the distant sky, I could see the Moon. As my eyes grew accustomed to the darkness, I could just about see my way. I thought back to what Selene had said last night about the word "lune" meaning mad. *Yeah, I must be mad to be doing this but, whatever, I have just found my inner lunatic,* I thought.

Keeping my back to the wall, I crept along until there was a window. There I fell to my knees so that, if anyone was looking out, they wouldn't see me. I crawled through some shrubs – not easy with the stupid duvet – and down to a path that led down through some woods. Along the way, I felt a nail break. *This is just the end!* I thought. *Can things possibly get any worse? I just pray that no-one I know ever finds out about this!* Once I'd reached the path, I stood up and looked around. I couldn't see any lights in the distance or sign of habitation at all – just the black silhouette of trees and hills as far as the eye could see. Mr O had said that it was remote, but there was *bound* to be something somewhere if I went far enough. There had to be.

A quick glance back to ensure that I hadn't been spotted, then I headed for the trees.

I ran for about fifteen minutes, keeping parallel to the path leading away from the boot camp, but I made sure that I was hidden by the trees. *Thank God that there's a little bit of light from the Moon,* I thought as I panted along next to the path, which seemed to go on for ever and ever without actually getting anywhere. I cursed the fact that we'd arrived in the dark last night, as if it had been daylight I might have been able to gauge exactly how far I was from people. And rescue.

I ran on, stopping for breath every now and again. It didn't look as if anyone was following, so I slowed my pace. I so wished I had eaten that sandwich and apple last night. I was *starving. I will probably die soon*, I thought. *Then they'll all be sorry.*

"Starving with broken nails, thanks a lot, Mum and Dad," I yelled at the sky, then realized that maybe that wasn't such a good idea. Someone might have heard me. I thought about all the chocolate bars I'd stashed in my suitcase and my mouth watered. I was sooooooooo hungry and thirsty. A spot of water splashed down on my face. Another spot. And another. And then the heavens opened and it began to rain.

Oh very funny, God, yeah, add to the fun and make it rain, why don't you? I thought as I made a dash under the thickest branches I could see to shelter. But it was to no avail. It was December and the trees were bare. The duvet I had wrapped around me wasn't waterproof, so was soon heavy with rain. A wave of anger flooded through me. Cold and hungry and thirsty in the dark and NOW WET! How *could* my mum and dad *do* this to me? I was going to die. I knew it. I was lost in the forest in the middle of nowhere. Like Little Red Riding Hood. *Oh God, I hope there aren't wolves around*, I thought. *Oh God oh God. I might get eaten by wild animals and then crows will come and peck at my carcass. And no-one will miss me until it's too late. Mum and Dad think I'm at the boot camp, tucked up in my dorm, not lost in the middle of nowhere. Oh God. They'll read about my death in the paper. Hah! THEN they'll be doubly sorry. Oh yeah.*

An image of my funeral flashed through my mind. Tigsy would be there, of course, wearing something fabulous with great big black shades. She'd be followed by Coco, whose fur would have been dyed black for the occasion. My little Coco. She'd miss me. *Oh, what should I do?* I asked myself. I looked to the left then to the right. In front. *Where should I go? Which way? How long can a person actually last without fries and a milk-shake and a decent manicure?*

I plonked myself onto the ground. I so wished I could talk to Tigsy. Or Poppy. At the thought of Poppy, I felt overwhelmingly sad. She loved me. She really did. She followed me around from the day she was born. Her big sister. Her hero. And then the very time she'd needed me most, I'd let her down. I stood up and slapped my arms to keep warm. *Mustn't think about her. Mustn't. Mustn't. Too too painful.* And then I wondered if these were the painful feelings that Mr O had warned me about in his note, the ones that the Moon would bring up? *No. No way. He couldn't know about my sister or about what I really felt deep, deep inside.*

And then I heard the roar of... what was it? Thunder? *Oh no.* Where there was thunder, there was lightning. I might get struck by it if the storm came closer. But no. It wasn't thunder. It was… I could see a headlight coming up the drive. It was a motorbike. I made up my mind in an instant. I couldn't stay out here in this weather a moment longer. I'd have to revert to plan B to escape. The fact that I hadn't got a plan B was beside the point. I'd come up with one all in good time. For the moment though, I needed to get dry.

I hopped out of the trees and flagged down the bike. The rider slowed down and came to a stop. As I approached, I saw that it was the cute boy-babe messenger, Hermie.

"Been running away, have you?" he asked.

I nodded. "Five stars for observation."

He ignored the sarcasm in my voice. "Ready to go back?"

A rivulet of rainwater dripped down my forehead and along my nose as I nodded again.

"Hop on," he said.

I did as I was told and a second later, just as Hermie revved the bike, a man stepped out from behind a tree.

"WaaAHH!" I almost leapt out of my skin with fear. And then I saw that it was that idiot from last night. The one who thought the sun shone out of his backside.

"Morning, Mr O," said Hermie.

"Morning," replied Mr O. He looked very dapper in a fabulous long black leather coat and black baseball cap. *How very* Matrix, I thought as I recalled the outfits in the movie. I had to hand it to Mr O, that although clearly out of his mind, he did have a certain sense of style. Not that I was about to let him know that though. He looked as if he had a big-enough ego as it was without me paying him compliments.

"I... I... You were there, behind me, all the time? I didn't hear you." I said.

He flashed his grin. "I was playing a part. Don't forget that I am an actor."

"And which part was that, then? A tree?"

Mr O looked offended. "Of course not. I was being the invisible man. *I* thought I'd done it rather well."

"Bu... why didn't you let me know that you were there or try to stop me?"

"I had to let you get it out of your system, Leonora. You're a Leo. A fire sign. They never take things lying down, so you were bound to try to escape at least once."

"I wonder why? And why were you following me?"

He pointed at himself and then at me. "Me guardian, you Zodiac Girl, remember? What kind of guardian do you think I am?"

"Oh don't start with the Zodiac Girl thing again..."

"But I have to. I am here to watch over you. Like the sun over a garden of flowers ready to bloom."

"Erg. Pardon me while I puke," I said. "You don't

need to bother. I don't need you."

Hermie took a sharp intake of breath as if I'd taken a step too far. He glanced at Mr O. I noted that the vein in his forehead was throbbing again. He looked at Hermie.

"Tough little minx, isn't she?" he said. "Leo, Leo, lovely Leo." He took a few deep breaths then turned to me with a cheerful expression that looked well fake. "Okay, little madam. Off you go. Go back and get dry while I go and... spread a little light around. Yes, that's what I'll do." With that, he turned back off the path and disappeared into the trees muttering something about having "Never seen anything like her in my life. Ungrateful little ma..."

Seconds later, I was roaring back up the drive as the sun rose behind us. *Back to the hotel from hell,* I thought as I clung on to Hermie's waist.

Chapter Eight

Brekkie

After Hermie dropped me off, I went straight to the dining area. I sooooo needed some breakfast like I'd never needed breakfast before. Plus I needed to keep my strength up for later when the right moment for escape presented itself. My stomach was making strange gurgling nosies, I was so utterly starving. I'd even eat a green apple if there was one. And that wholemeal bread too, if they didn't have croissants. But they were bound to have croissants. Everyone did.

I vaguely remembered where the dining room was from my tour with Mr O and soon found the others in there gloomily tucking into what looked like beige gloop in plastic bowls, while Selene stood behind an enormous pan on a table at the back of the room. She was dressed in a long silver dress and looked like a fairy queen and well out of place in the dismal room where the air smelt of boiled cloth. *Ah, happy days*, I thought as I glanced around. *Not.*

"Eew. What is that disgusting stuff?" I asked Jake, who was sitting nearest the door.

"Boiled glue," he said.

"Porridge," said Lynn.

"Tastes like glue," said Jake and he faked his teeth being glued together by it so that he could only chew in slow motion. I almost laughed, but then remembered that I was very, *very* cross and unhappy.

At that moment, Dr Cronus came in and Jake immediately put his bowl on his head, made himself go cross-eyed and started making a noise like a police car. Porridge dripped down his forehead.

I almost laughed again. I could get to like Jake. Poppy would have liked him if she'd been here. One of the best things about her was that she was a giggler and always laughed easily, even when people's jokes weren't that funny. She'd have been on the floor at Jake's antics.

The doctor glanced over at him, but didn't even blink an eye.

"Most amusing, boy," he said. "It's not working though. I know that you're as sane as I am."

"Which isn't very sane," I whispered, "because according to Mr O, all the staff here think that they're planets, so basically, they've all outluned you."

"Umbongo banana," said Jake and leapt up onto the table and went into a monkey impersonation. I hoped that he was still doing his madness act because, if he wasn't, he was *very* weird.

Dr Cronus seemed to be counting that we were all present, then he left the room. I went over to the table where Selene was dolling out the gloop.

"I'll have a chocolate croissant and a hot chocolate," I said.

"Will you now? Yes. Well, that *sounds* nice, but we don't have anything like that. This is all there is." And she picked up a ladleful of porridge then let it slop back into the pan with a splot sound.

Although the gloop looked disgusting, my stomach was rumbling so much that I decided that I had to give in *just* this once. I had had porridge once in a hotel in Scotland and, if you put enough sugar and fruit on it, it can taste *just* about all right.

"Okay, give me some, but with loads of maple syrup and cream and some peaches."

"I can't do that," she said. She put the lid on the pan then reached below the counter, found a plastic cup, filled it with water from the tap behind her and handed it to me.

"What's this?"

"Your breakfast. Tap water."

"Er, excuse me. Reality check. I don't drink tap water. Okay, I did last night, but that was all you gave me. I don't drink just any old brand of water, but *tap* water? And from a plastic cup? I only drink from china and crystal. Now cut out the antics and give me some porridge and put it in a DECENT bowl."

"Suit yourself," she said and put the cup back down.

"Isn't there any hot chocolate or cappuccino or something hot?" I asked.

Mark snorted behind me.

"Get 'er," said Marilyn and went into a mimic of me. "Oo get me an 'ot chocolate, slave. Oi, 'edley Bent. Sit down and shurrup, you poncy git."

"You'll get a cup of tea if you're lucky," said Lynn.

"I don't want tea. I *want* porridge," I said through gritted teeth, although a part of me couldn't believe I was demanding a bowl of what looked like slug slime.

"Say please," said Selene. "It's nice to be nice."

I rolled my eyes. "Please," I said wearily. *Honestly,* I thought, *these people, they don't half take life seriously.*

"No," said Selene.

"No? But... I just said please."

"Mario said no breakfast for giving him cheek earlier this morning and that you have to learn respect. It's in your birth chart. Major lesson to learn. That and must get in touch with her real feelings and not hold everything in until there's an explosion."

"Oh really? You think that I must learn respect, do you? Get in touch with my feelings? I don't think so. I've seen birth charts. They're all lines and squiggles and angles in a circle. Nothing about respect and no breakfast for naughty Leos. Come on Moonface, give us a break."

"No. Can't. No porridge."

Behind me, Marilyn laughed. I didn't like being laughed at and she was beginning to annoy me. Before Selene could stop me, I lifted the lid off the porridge pan, ladled out a bowlful and scooped some up into my hand. It felt *dis*gusting, like puréed snail *and* it was cold, but I didn't care. I turned around and hurled it at Marilyn. It hit her, splat, right in the face and began to drip slowly over her forehead.

"I've HAD enough of you," I said. "You might talk rot about being a murderer and you might scare some weedy stupid people, but you DON'T scare me."

"Warghhhh, splah… wur…" Marilyn blustered through the lumpy goo. She wiped a little from her eyes while the rest slid down her cheeks and onto her navy fleece. "Right, posh ponce. You asked for it." She stood up and was about to come towards me.

With the fingers of both my hands, I beckoned her to try it. "Bring it on," I said as I reached in and armed myself with another handful of gunk and looked at Selene. "Hey. You said to get in touch with my feelings, Moon Girl."

"Oh. Oh dear. I should have known," said Selène. "New moon. At an awkward angle to Mars. People's emotions are always heightened. There was bound to be some kind of fight. Oh. Er… come on now, dears. Play nice."

I threw a handful of porridge over her too and watched with satisfaction as it dripped over her forehead and onto her lovely silver dress. *So what? What a stupid thing to be wearing in a place like this,* I thought. And anyway, she had been annoying me too, with her lovey-dovey manner, ever since the moment I'd clapped eyes on her.

"Yahay! Food fight," yelled Jake, and in a split second he was standing next to me filling his hands with porridge.

Dr Cronus appeared at the door. "What's all the commotion? I—" Splot. Jake hit the old man with porridge on his arm then punched the air with glee. "Result! Excellent." Old Croniepoo dodged out of the way and out the door. Selene followed swiftly behind him.

"Chickens," I called after them, then I tucked my hands under my arms and did a little chicken dance. Jake joined in with me.

"Bec, bec, berk, berk, perk," we clucked.

In a flash, the others were at the table and all of them had handfuls of porridge which they were chucking at each other like it was a snowball fight. For a moment, it almost felt like fun and reminded me of a time when Poppy and I had had a food fight. It was when she was six and we'd thrown chocolate cake mix around. Even Mum and Dad joined in. That was when we were still a happy family. That was a long time ago.

Splat. Splat. Splot. Porridge was being fired everywhere.

And then we heard the door blast open and a very loud whistle.

I stopped mid hurl and glanced over to see a very angry-looking Mario standing there. He was dressed in a wet suit complete with snorkel *and* flippers, and he was carrying a megaphone. He looked so totally ridiculous that I burst out laughing, but the others stopped what they were doing immediately.

"STEP AWAY from the porridge," said Mario through the megaphone. "STEP *away* from the porridge."

I couldn't stop laughing, but the others didn't seem to find it as funny.

"Mouldy bananas," groaned Lynn. "There goes our hot water for the next week."

"Yeah," snarled Jake, then he looked in my direction. "And it's all your fault."

Marilyn pointed at me. "Yeah. She started it, sir. She's the troublemaker."

I gave a little curtsey and held up a handful of gloop. "Yeah. Because I AM ZODIAC GIRL, don't you know? A rare honour I'm told. Anyone like to see what I do as an ENCORE?"

"Out," commanded Mario. "*All* of you. Assemble in the hall."

Jake, Mark, Lynn and Marilyn filed out. I stood my ground. I wasn't going anywhere.

"That means you too, missy."

"Since when did I take orders from you?"

"Since I was told that you were this month's Zodiac Girl and I saw your chart..."

I sighed. "Oh here we go again. I told you, I don't want to be a Zodiac Girl. I can assure it's not the honour you think it is. Least not so far... Are the others Zodiac Girls and boys too?"

"Nope. Just you."

"So why me?"

"It's in your stars. You got one month here. Make the most of it. Now MOVE your sorry butt. We're going to hose you all down in the bathroom. With ice-COLD water. That will show you."

"Not me. No way." I decided to show him what I could do if I had a tantrum. I could cause trouble. He'd soon see it would be in his best interests not to get on the wrong side of me. The others might be pussycats, but not this girl. Not *Zodiac* Girl. Ooooh no. Not me.

I roared as loud as I could. Like a lion.

"ReeeeOOOOOOOOOOOOOOAAAAAR!!!"

Mr O popped his head around the door when I did that and nodded as if he approved of what he heard. "That's my little Leo. Yes. Yes. Let it all out. Roar like a lion, Leonora. All out. Yes. Good. Fine." And then he disappeared.

I pushed the porridge pan over; I kicked the table; I poured water out of all the cups. I hurled a chair at the wall. Roaring all the time. "I DON'T WANT TO BE HERE. YOU CAN'T MAKE ME STAY. I WON'T EAT YOUR PORRIDGE. AND I WON'T DO WHAT YOU TELL ME. AND I DON'T WANT TO BE ZODIAAAAAAAAAAC GIRL."

At one point I glanced over at him to see how upset Mario looked. He wasn't *even* watching! He was looking out the window as if there was something more *interesting* going on out there! I. Could. Not. Believe. It. So I picked up the nearest bowl and threw it at him, being careful that it went over his shoulder and hit the wall (I didn't want to get him too angry), but close enough to make him look. He did duck, but he didn't seem worried.

I threw a few more bowls at the walls and being plastic they bounced off, not that Mario cared. He was looking out the window again. And then he got a newspaper out from somewhere in his wet suit, sat down, crossed his legs and began reading it like he was sitting outside a café in the south of blooming France! I looked around to see what else I could trash from the mess in front of me, but I seemed to have thrown just about everything I could.

"Finished?" asked Mario after a while.

I surveyed the destruction in front of me and felt smug. *Good job,* I thought. *That will show him not to mess with me.* "Yeah. I think I might have done. Now. Let that be a lesson to you."

Mario pointed at a cupboard in the corner of the room. "To me? Oh no. I don't think so. Dr Cronus definitely said that the lesson was yours this morning. So. Mops in there. Buckets are in there, too. Washing-up liquid, cleaning fluids are at the back of the kitchen under the sinks. Now you clear up this mess and, when the place is ship-shape, you can move on."

My stomach suddenly growled a really loud growl, reminding me that I hadn't eaten since yesterday.

"But... I... I haven't even had any breakfast."

"And who's to blame for that, do you think? Who made this mess? It's in your horoscope that you have to learn that actions have consequences, so you aren't going to get anything to eat until you've cleared up what you've done in here. You get me?"

"Isn't there anything NICE in my horoscope?"

"Depends on how you play it. What you make of what life gives you."

"Pff. Where's Mr O? He's supposed to be my guardian. I'm sure he wouldn't like it if you didn't feed me." I pouted. It was worth a try. I used to be able to wind Daddy round my little finger when I pouted, although that was a long time ago.

"Mr O has left the premises for the time being. He isn't too happy with the way you've rejected him, I can tell you that much, so don't be expecting any help from him too soon, not unless you change your attitude, that is. You get me?"

I went to kick a wall.

"Uh-uh… I think you get me all right," he said, and walked over to the door where he produced a key. "Now what you probably need is some chill time, so I'm going to give you that. Think things over while you're in here. You like it or not, you're going to stay here at this lodge until we say you can go, and either you play along and make life sweet, or you be difficult and you make life hard. Your choice. Always will be."

"Bully."

"I'm no bully. And I'm not the one who had the tantrum here. Now there's water in the tap there if you get thirsty and," he got up and had a look in the bottom of the pan, " there's just a scraping of porridge left, too. In the meantime, the sooner you clear up, the sooner you get out of here."

My answer was to pick up another bowl and throw it at him as he left the room. Once again it missed and hit the door as it closed behind him, leaving me alone in a porridge-covered room.

There was only one thing for it and I took a deep breath and let rip. "Er... WAGHHHHHHHHHH." I yelled. "WAAAAAAAAAAAAAAAAAAAAAAAAAAAA-AAAAAAAAAAAAAAAAAAAAAAAAAAAAAgh."

I waited. Someone was *bound* to come when they heard that. It was awesome, even by my standards. Someone *always* came running when I really let rip. But no. Not even the sound of a footstep creeping to the door to listen to what I was up to as had happened so often when I'd had a tantrum at my old schools.

I picked up a chair and hurled it against the door. It kebonged back into the room as, like the bowls, even the furniture was made of plastic. I made a good commotion, though. *That ought to bring them running,* I thought.

Nothing.

I tried wailing again. I really did feel mad. But once again – nothing. It was as if they'd forgotten about me. Or lost interest.

Outside, it was starting to get lighter. I ran to the window and looked out. We were in the middle of nowhere. In front was a landscape of hills and fields, shrubs and trees.

It was my first day. I'd been up barely two hours and it wasn't even eight o'clock yet. How on earth was I going to survive for a whole month here?

Chapter Nine

Routine

I soon got into the routine. *Not* that they had won. I had no choice, not if I was going to survive, and I *am* a survivor. It was play along and be their little Zodiac Girl or starve. Play along or freeze. Play along or be even more miserable than I was on my first night and I thought at the time that *that* took the prize. But I was wrong. Things got worse and my time in hell was like this:

5.30 a.m. Wake-up call. Get up. Yeah. Five-thirty in the morning!!!!! I used to think that there was only one five-thirty in the day and that was in the afternoon. Now I knew different. Every morning there was a little note from Mr O explaining various aspects of my birth chart and how they were going to appear that day. In other words, outlining what nasty surprises I had in store – there certainly weren't any perks to being a Zodiac Girl, that was for sure.

5.30 – 6 a.m. Wash. For the first time in my life, I have to share soap and toothpaste. It was *so* disgusting. The soap smells of antiseptic. Yerk. I was *sooooo* missing my Goddess products. The most mortifying thing, though, was the first time I washed my hair. There was no conditioner and then Mario wouldn't let me get my straightening iron from my suitcase, which was still locked away.

"Let it dry naturally," he said, so revealing just how cruel a torturer he was.

I felt like my world had come to an end. Curly hair. I'd rather die. In the end I had no option but to let it dry on its own but I shoved it back into a plait before anyone could see how horrible it looked. Then I wore my uniform baseball cap to cover it up further. And mean Selene wouldn't give me any solution for my blue contacts so I had to go *au naturel*. Brown eyes. And my nails. I can't even look at the sorry sight they have become after a week of no manicures. There was *no* end to my shame.

6 – 7 a.m. Breakfast – if you could call it that but I had to eat *some*thing. Each night I dreamt of freshly baked croissants and home-made raspberry jam, blueberry muffins, cheese toasties and Danish pastries with hot chocolate. Sadly, dreams don't satisfy your hunger, so I had to eat what there was. Of all the things in this boot camp, having to eat horse food is the second worst (curly hair is the first).

7 – 8 a.m. Hike around the grounds. Truly. Some

days it was raining, one day it even snowed, but that didn't stop old Sergeant Macho Mario making us march like we were his personal army. And not just march. He made all of us carry heavy backpacks. Every day. In all kind of weathers. The CHEEK of it. It was completely and utterly and totally the most miserable activity I had ever done in my entire life. But there was no getting out of it. Not if I wanted to live. Or eat. Or sleep with a pillow.

One day, I pretended to play along with the "planets here as people" idea and I asked Mario how many planets there were in astrology and how many were here in physical form. "Ten," he replied. I did my maths. I'd met only five of them. I surmised that the other five might be nicer. Mario said that they could be if you got them on the right day, but they weren't predominant in my chart this month. He has a sneaky answer for everything. I sooo hate him.

8 – 10 a.m. Chores. Yeah. Me, Leonora Hedley-Dent had to do chores. Cleaning. Peeling potatoes. Polishing furniture. And actually it was something to do and made the long days go quicker.

10 – 12 noon. Lessons with Dr Croniebum. I don't really know what he was droning on about most days as I tuned him out. More about the ten planets, but I wasn't interested since Mario had told me the other five (Venus, Uranus, Neptune, Pluto and Jupiter) weren't going to appear like superheroes to make things better. Dr Cronus could make me sit there, but I didn't have to take it in. All that stuff that Mr O had been on about on the first night, about me being a Zodiac Girl, as far as I was concerned, it was a one-way ticket to Loserville.

12 – 1 p.m. Lunch. Lunch! Hah. Usually soup and a bit of bread. If you were lucky and hadn't had the "privilege" taken away.

1 – 4 p.m. Gardening. Back out in all the elements. Raking leaves. Digging over flower beds. My hands got blisters on them from the spades and did anyone care? Not a bit.

4 – 6 p.m. Counselling with Miss Bongo from Bongoland herself, Selene Luna in the dining room. She had a variety of methods which entailed dancing about like trees and pretending to be the sea. I asked her what the point of that was and she said it was to get in touch with the free spirit, the nature child that lives within us all. I told her and her nature child to take a running jump off the nearest cliff, which made Jake laugh a lot. He seems to think I am very funny – like a natural comedian. Pff. Just shows what he knows. I was being *deadly* serious.

Another task she got us to do was to walk about the room with a partner while one of you closes their eyes and the other guides. She said it was to encourage working as a team – something that I needed to learn having seen in my birth chart that I was as a double Leo who wanted my own way. *Birth chart, smurf chart,* I thought as I steered Mark into a wall – he got a nosebleed.

Well, serves him right. The silence thing he does annoys me. Lynn had filled me in on his story. She was good for all the goss. His dad had lost his job a couple of years ago and his family were poor, so he got into shoplifting so that his family could eat and his younger sister could have presents on birthdays and at Christmas. *Like, boo hoo, not my problem,* I thought.

They were a bunch of losers. All their problems stemmed from being broke, including Marilyn's. Her story was no biggie either. Her dad had left. It was an ugly divorce and her mum and Marilyn had to move out of their posh house and live in a smaller place. Worst thing for her, according to Lynn, was not being able to wear her designer gear any more as they couldn't afford it. *Now that I can relate to,* I thought as Lynn filled me in on the rest of the story about how Marilyn had become "difficult" and started acting the tough girl at school. Hah! I could show her difficult at school! I *knew* that murder hadn't even come into it! She was just a classic case of the divorce doldrums and I'd seen a hundred of those. *Saddo,* I thought. At my old school, you were the odd one out if your parents were still *together*. In Lynn's case, her dad had died and her mum remarried. She didn't like her stepdad so she rebelled, and, like me had been expelled from her last school.

"Sometimes I wish I'd done it differently," she confessed one night after we'd collapsed into bed. "I'm not totally stupid and I can see that, in the end, the person who's suffered most is me. Changing schools meant leaving mates and now I ain't got any. Sometimes I feel lonely. In fact being in 'ere is the closest I've got to 'aving mates in ages."

"I know what you mean," I said. "I've lost a lot of friends along the way, too. My best mate is my little dog now. Coco."

Lynn smiled. "I've always wanted a pet. My mum always promised I could 'ave one if I behaved. Trouble was, I never did."

Jake's background was the saddest of all. He had a younger brother who was ill and all the family's money went on medical bills. Jake had stolen a car and tried to sell it to raise funds. I *almost* felt sorry for him and the others when their tales of woe came out, but I steeled myself and put up an inner wall just in time. Reminded myself that I didn't let anyone get too close. It only caused pain if I did. I knew that from past experience. And anyhow, I could fix their problems in a second by lending them some dosh from my private savings account. I'd ask for interest, of course. It could all be so easily sorted. I even offered at a return plus twenty per cent which I thought was quite generous considering the circumstances.

None of them took up the offer, so I pushed down the sympathy I'd fleetingly felt for them. All their problems could be resolved. Not like mine. None of their stories was as tragic as mine, but they'd never get to hear it, not one of them, not even Lynn.

6 – 7 p.m. Supper, which was rice and vegetables or baked potato and vegetables. Vegetables! Yeee-uck. I so don't do vegetables. Or at least didn't used to. I used to think that broccoli was for losers. And now I have to eat it most nights because, if I don't, I'd get nothing else. I tried not to think about Tigsy and the stay I missed at the fabocious hotel in Paris. She'd have been eating the best of everything. Dinky dishes on divine designer plates, not this plastic rubbish they use here. And to *think* of some of the meals I had sent back because they were too cold or too hot or too slimy! I'd *kill* for them now. Even an avocado would be welcome.

7 – 10 p.m. Recreation time, meaning more misery in the way of sports activities and workshops, sometimes with Mr O and sometimes with Macho Mario. No *real* recreation. Like shopping. Or TV. Or eating chocolate or anything that reminded me of home. Mr O was distinctly cooler with me after the first day when I tried to run away, and he kept muttering under his breath about "a waste of time," and "never in all his days had he met with such ingratitude." *Pfff*, I thought. *He is so used to being the centre of attention, which is why he doesn't like it if someone disses him.*

I went along with the routine because I had to, although every day felt like it lasted an eternity. I *even* had to ask permission to go to the bathroom! But there was no escape. I played along and they thought I'd given in. Idiots! As if. I hadn't. Not in my head I hadn't. Someone would pay. And when I got out, I'd soon show Mum and Dad how much their little betrayal had *really* cost them!

Of course I did my best to rebel in the first couple of days. Every trick in the book. But these guys were good, they were *very* good and it was going to take me some time to work out how to get the better of them. I tried feigning a heart attack, a vomit attack, headache, migraine, but they just yawned like they'd seen it all before and – having witnessed Jake's nut-boy antics and Mark's prolonged silence, I guessed that they had.

In the first week, I went without some meals – like when I discovered I had to actually help cook the food. All I said when asked to chop some onions was "Excuse me, do I look like anyone's slave?" and I wasn't allowed any dinner! My clothes soon began to feel looser through lack of food.

I went without my pillows as a punishment for running away on my first day and I went without hot water for starting the porridge fight, which was *so* unfair because I did clean up in the end – after about eight hours, in fact, which is something of a record for getting me to do something.

For the first three days, Mario insisted that I was kept apart from the others and made me sit in a stone circle in the main hallway. On my own. For hours on end. He told me that he was actually being kind because some inmates had to sit in a stone circle *outside* in the cold and that's what I'd have to do if I didn't co-operate. And that's when I decided I'd play along for a while. It was soooooooooooo booooooooooooring in that stupid circle, but being chucked out into the freezing December weather would have been even worse. I finally had to give in and say, whatever. I decided that I would play the game. Whatever it took to get out of here and back to my normal life.

Some evenings there were more messages from Mr O at the end of my bed. Always about the stars, stuff like – today Mars has been at an angle to Saturn. Or, Pluto was square to the Sun or trident or sextile – with bits of advice thrown in. I asked the others again about the zodiac thing and they knew nothing about it. None of them was a Zodiac Girl or Boy, that was for sure. Seeing as they were my only allies in there, I didn't pursue it. I didn't want to be any more of an odd girl out than I already was. I acted like I was going along with it to Mr O though, and smiled and thanked him for his kind messages – then I tore them up and put them in the bin.

One thing I swore to myself and that was that no-one would see me cry. I'd never let them know that they had upset me. And one of these days, I would get my revenge. And *then* they'd be sorry.

One of the weekly tasks in counselling was to write a letter home. My first one went like this:

GET ME OUT *OF HERE!!! NOW!!!!!*

But then Lunie Pants Selene took a look at it and told me that I had to do it again. "Dig deep, my little flower," she said. "Tell them how you really feel."

So I wrote this:

Mum and Dad, (I wrote Dear Mum and Dad then realized that they *weren't* dear, not to me. Not any more. So I crossed the "dear" out.) *GET ME OUT OF HERE NOW!!!! I HATE YOU. I am locked up with a bunch of crazy people who think that they are stars!!!*

That letter got vetoed as well.

"You asked me to tell dig deep and I did," I said. "That's how I feel."

Lunie made me do a third one.

Mr and Mrs Hedley-Dent,

I have been instructed that I have to write you a letter as a weekly task. I do this under pressure, like everything else in this cold miserable godforsaken place, because I have learned that if I don't do as I am told then I am punished or starved. I HATE you more than ever and can't believe you have made me suffer in this way. When I get out of this prison sentence you have put me through, I will be going to live with someone else. I disown you as my parents. And I will sell my story to the papers so that everyone knows what horrible people you are. And then you'll be sorry. So there.

Look after Coco.

From Leonora Hedley-Dent

"I am soooo going to make my parents pay for this," I said to Lynn at the end of week one as we went to the gym for sports activities.

"Yeah," she said. "In the meantime, though, I wonder what torture Mario has lined up for us this evening."

We didn't have to wait long to find out. Mr O came jogging around the corner. He looked ridiculous. He was dressed in a white tracksuit with what looked like a white cashmere scarf tossed casually around his neck. His trainers were pure white too, like they'd never been worn outside. With his dazzling good looks, he always looked like he was about to go into a photo shoot for a men's catalogue – not a hair out of place, his teeth brighter than bright, his skin so tanned it was almost orange.

"Hedley-Dent, you're with me," he said. "The rest of you, Mario said meet him out front for a night hike."

"Oh noooooooooo," groaned Jake. "Not again."

"Fresh air is good for the soul," said Mr O, who then indicated that I should follow him. I slouched along behind him as he led me into the gym and flicked on the lights. Hanging from the ceiling was what looked like an enormous sausage.

"*What* is that?" I asked.

Mr O flashed his kilowatt smile. "*That* is whatever you want it to be."

"Ah. So it's a private plane to get me out of here?"

"No need to be sarcastic, Leonora. Didn't you get my zodiac message this morning?"

I shrugged. "Yeah." Like all the messages, I had cast a cursory glance over it before putting it in the bin. It had said something about the Moon being square to Mars.

"Emotions that are hard to express can manifest in anger or impatience, especially for a Leo. I'm going to show you another way to get them out."

"Whatever," I said and pointed back at the sausage thing. "So. What is it?"

"It's a punchbag."

"You're going to teach me to box?"

"Not exactly."

"So what then?"

"Go and give it a bash and you'll see," he said. "I'll show you how."

He pranced off towards the bag and starting taking jabs at it in the way that you see boxers doing when in training for a fight. After a few minutes, he stopped, went to the equipment cupboard at the back of the gym, pulled out a pair of boxing gloves and tossed them to me. "Your turn."

I put on the gloves, approached the bag and gave it a tap.

"Put some *elbow* into it, girl," commanded Mr Razzle Dazzle.

I gave it another tap.

"Nooooo, like this," said Mr O as he ran towards the bag and whacked it. "Come on Leonora. *Go* for it."

I gave it a few more half-hearted taps. Like, boxing is so last decade. "Okay. Okay. I'm doing it. I'm doing it."

Mr O started prancing around me making little jabby punching motions. "Hit it, go on. Hit it."

He was starting to annoy me. I hit the bag with a little more force.

"*That's* more like it. Come on. Let's get a little energy up here. Come *ON*. Show me what you're made of."

I stopped and yawned. "I am *so* not interested in this.

Like, give me a break. You're supposed to be my guardian, aren't you? Don't I get some time off for good behaviour? Time off for being Zodiac Girl or whatever?"

"This *is* your time off. You could be out there hiking with the others."

"Oo. Pardon me if I don't fall over with gratitude."

"Pardoned," said Mr O and flashed me a grin.

"I was being sarcastic."

"So was I."

He started ducking and diving around me, pretending I was the punchbag, although he didn't touch me. Jab, jab. It was getting very, *very* annoying. "Go on punch the bag, *punch* the bag."

So I did. I *really* punched it.

Mr O continued dancing behind me. "Excellent. Now. Who makes you mad?"

"You do."

"Then pretend I'm the bag."

I did. And I whacked the bag with all my might.

Jab, jab. Mr O continued around my head like he was a fly, buzzing round. Jab, jab, buzz, buzz. "Now who else annoys you?"

"*All* of you here."

"Great. Good. Now pretend the bag is Dr Cronus."

I whacked it. "Take that old Wiz Woz."

"Wiz Woz?"

"Yeah. Cronus looks like an old wizard."

"I guess he does. Now. Do Selene," said Mr O, all the while continuing to dance around me in a circle, jabbing the air with his clenched fists.

I whacked the bag again. "And you, Miss Hippie Happy Clappy."

Mr O snorted with laughter. "Hippie Happy Clappy. Hah! And your mum and dad. You're mad at them, aren't you."

He was talking fast and spinning round me in circles and, when he mentioned Mum and Dad, I felt the rage I'd been holding back all week while I'd been doing my Miss Play-along role rise to the surface. I began to hit the bag. Whack. Whack. Thwack.

Mr O was gleeful and punched the air. "Who else? Who else?"

"Henry. Grrrrrr." Mr O didn't have to encourage me this time. I'd got the hang of it and, once I'd started, I couldn't stop. It was like a tsunami of rage was flooding through me and I was helpless to stop it. "WAAAAAAAAAAAAAAGHHH!"

I whacked Henry with all I'd got. Then Shirla for not coming with me on the plane. And Mr Nash at my last school for expelling me. And Mrs Simons. And Headmaster Ericson. And Polly James in my last dorm. And... There was a long list of contenders lining up in my head to have their faces imprinted on the punchbag. I went for it. Punch. Thwack. Punch. Thwack. And a few kicks for good measure. Thwackawackawacka-wackawack. I whacked away until there was no more whack inside of me. I was whacked out. I bent over to catch my breath. I was red in the face. And perspiring. And then *she* was there, a face at the end of the queue of people to be mad with. I took a sharp intake of breath and pushed her back to the recesses of my mind. But she'd been there for a second. Mo Bolton. Looming up like an ominous shadow with that snide look that she'd always had when she sensed a fight was about to happen.

Mr O seemed to sense that I'd reached some kind of wall or door inside of myself. "Enough?"

I held up a hand. "Enough."

"Take a few breaths, Leonora," said Mr O, then he added gently. "You did good. You did really good."

And the strange thing was, I *felt* good, just for a few seconds. Like I'd released something from deep inside of me.

And then suddenly I felt very tired. I crumpled to the floor and lay with my arms out like a cross. Mo mustn't be allowed out. I mustn't even think of her. What she did. And even worse, what she made *me* do to Poppy.

Chapter Ten

Bah humbug!

It was December 24th, Christmas Eve and just after breakfast. I'd been at the funny farm for almost three miserable, stinking weeks. Mr O had left his usual note this morning, something about Saturn and Pluto and restrictions. I don't know why he bothered. The messages didn't make any sense. Plus there had been a bit about Mars moving into Aquarius which would bring about a more relaxed feeling and Jupiter putting in an appearance. *Like ding dong merrily on high,* I thought. *Relaxed about being here over Christmas? Was that supposed to make me feel better?* I was counting down the days. Counting down the hours. Counting down the minutes until I could get out of there and back to my life.

We'd just finished our bowls of gloop and I'd been trying not to imagine what I would have been having for breakfast if I was at home (fresh almond pastries flown in from a little deli in Belgium, fresh raspberries with fresh cream with a hot chocolate), when Mario appeared with boxes of Christmas decorations.

He spilled tinsel, red and gold stars and baubles out onto the table. "Mark, Jake, you two go out into the grounds and cut holly and ivy. Girls, you make a start in the hall."

I'd behaved myself for three weeks and today I wasn't in the mood. I picked up the last spoon of porridge and turned it over so that it fell back into my bowl with a splat. "D'er. Why?" I asked without looking up.

"To make it festive," he said.

"Do it yourself," I said, putting down my spoon and crossing my arms. "Like what did your last slave die of?"

"What did your last slave die of," Mario mimicked. "Not that routine again. Come on, Hedley-Dent, if you're going to insult me, for heaven's sake come up with something new. In the meantime, decorations, Christmas, the season to be jolly. Let's do it."

"The others can, but count me out."

"It's a team task," said Mario. "We'll all muck in."

"Not me."

"And pray, why not?"

"I don't do Christmas."

Mark, Jake, Lynn and Marilyn were all watching the exchange like they were watching a tennis match.

"Ah," said Mario. "You might not, but we do."

"Listen, soldier boy," I said. "You might not have

noticed but I have been brought here against my will. I have been separated from my parents. And so far I have played along. Hiked when you said hike. Cleaned when you said clean. Jumped when you said jump. But decorate this hellhole? Forget it. As I said, I *don't* do Christmas. End of story."

Mario narrowed his eyes. "You either co-operate or take time out on your own to think things over."

"So bite me. You can't make me."

"I… think… it would be…. in your best interest to help with the decorations."

"And I *say* bah *humBUG*. What part of that do you *not* understand?"

"*What* is your problem, Hedley-Dent? Would you like to share it with the group?"

"Yeah. Sure. Mark, Jake, Lynn, Marilyn. I hate Christmas and everything that goes with it. I can't wait for it to be over. Okay. I've shared? Happy now?"

"Okay. Fair enough, but you have had it explained to you a thousand times," Mario droned on. "Three weeks you've been here and you still haven't got it. As with all exercises that are done as a team, your behaviour affects everyone else."

"What? So we all have to go and sit in your stupid stone circle?"

"No. Only you. But I'm giving you until five o'clock exactly. If you aren't ready to join in by then, your bad mood will affect the whole group."

"Yeah, like they care for one second what's happening with me."

"Oh I think that they will today," said Mario, "because if you don't come and join in, no supper. For anyone."

"That's not fair, sir," said Jake.

Mario turned to Jake and fixed him with a stare. "Did I give you permission to speak?"

"No, sir."

"Then be quiet. You were saying Hedley-Dent?"

"Ooooo, no supper, sir. Like there's anything to miss. A bit of mouldy old potato and carrot. They'll probably thank me."

"Ah no. Tonight is special. It's Christmas Eve and a friend of ours is bringing up a feast from the local deli."

"Yeah, right," I scoffed. "It's all part of the torture. You're teasing us."

"No. Didn't you read your horoscope this morning? About Jupiter?"

Lynn suddenly pointed out the window. "Ohmygod," she interrupted. "No. He's telling the truth. Look what's being unloaded out the back."

Jake, Mark and Marilyn got up and went to join her at the window. Jake punched the air. "Yesss! Get a load of that grub coming in!"

I waited a few moments, but then I got up and

sauntered over to the window, but I did it in a really casual way, to show that I wasn't really bothered.

Outside, the sky was dark with heavy black clouds but, sure enough, by the kitchen door was a big white van with the back doors wide open and a light on. A big, jolly-looking man was busy unloading boxes and platters. He had dark hair, but, in the right wig and beard, he was the sort who would have made an excellent Father Christmas.

"Come on, let's go to the kitchen," said Lynn, then glanced back at Mario. "Oh yeah. I mean... permission to go, sir?"

"Granted," said Mario.

Mark, Jake, Marilyn and Lynn sped off. Mario looked at me and raised an eyebrow as if to say, are you going to go too?

"Well, I might as well," I said as I got up to go with the others. "Anything's better than staying in here with you."

The first thing that hit me when I opened the kitchen door was the warmth coming from a roaring fire in the grate and a lovely smell of cinnamon and orange coming from a pan on the aga. The room had been transformed and felt delightfully festive. There was even music, carols playing out of hidden speakers, but, best of all, the long table was groaning with food fit for a banquet.

The jolly-looking man came in, put an enormous platter of the most scrummy-looking mince pies down and pointed at the aga. "I made some punch," he said. "My own special recipe. You all look like you could do with a bit of cheering up. Non-alcoholic of course. Help yourselves."

"Meet Joe," said Mario coming in behind me. "He runs a deli in a village not too far from here. Best chef in the land – in the world, in fact."

Joe nodded and beamed. "In the universe! *And* I'm the manifestation of Jupiter. Jupiter being the planet of expansion and jollity."

Lynn and Marilyn exchanged glances. "Nutter," said Lynn under her breath.

"Who cares?" commented Marilyn. "As long as we get some of that nosh."

"So where's the Zodiac Girl?" asked Joe.

"Zodiac Girl? What *is* this stuff about zodiacs?" asked Jake as he looked around. "Leonora mentioned it the other day. What's going on?"

I could see that Joe was about to come out with some nonsense similar to that which Mr O came out with, and I didn't want him drawing attention to me with any mad ramblings. I'd learned long ago that, if you're singled out as odd, you get picked on.

"I think it's some kind of club they're all in, like a zodiac club. Best play along with these crazy people especially if we're to get the grub," I whispered to Jake, Mark, Marilyn and Lynn, then I turned to Joe. "Yeah, yeah, me, them, we're all zodiac people here. Hello Jupiter. Welcome to the lodge. The grub looks good. Need a hand bringing it in?"

Joe raised an eyebrow and exchanged looks with Mario.

"She's a tough one," said Mario. "A double Leo."

"Ah," said Joe, and he rubbed his hands and gave me a wink. "Okay, guys. Help yourself to punch."

Jake was over by the pan in a flash and ladled out five cups of the hot amber liquid, which he handed around. I took my first sip and had to hold back from gasping with delight. It was the most divine drink I had ever tasted, spicy and sweet at the same time. If the food was as good as this, we were in for a real treat.

We drank the first cup, then Jake refilled our glasses and all the while Joe brought in more and more food. I thought I'd never seen anything more beautiful. An enormous turkey. Platters of sausages wrapped in bacon. Little mini pizzas. Roast potatoes. Pastries and cakes of every kind – iced and fruit, some with marzipan. Chocolate mousse. Trifle. A banoffee pie. *Oh bliss, layers of cream, toffee and banana, one of my favourites.* Great bunches of grapes. White and red. Strawberries. Raspberries. A platter of cheeses. Tubs of ice cream: toffee pecan, pistachio, toffee fudge, chocolate chip.

Bottles labelled: *maple syrup*, *chocolate sauce*, *vanilla melt*. And trays of sweets: liquorice all-sorts, jelly beans, jelly babies, dolly mixtures and chocolates of every shape and size.

My mouth began to water and I could see that the others were feeling the same. Mark was almost drooling.

"Thank you, God or Jupiter or Santa or whoever's up there," cried Jake and pointed to what looked like a pork pie. "Get a load of that big pie. Yeee-um. Bagsy that."

"So," said Mario coming up behind to join us, "Leonora, do you think that now you might join us in the team task of decorating?"

He must think I am such a pushover, I thought as I dragged my eyes away from a triple-layer vanilla slice that oozed custard.

"This is bribery," I said. "And it will all go in my story to the press."

"Oh knock it off," growled Marilyn. "Stop acting the brat princess. We're all starving and know that you are too. And you don't need to worry about being fat any more, cos you've got thinner in the past few weeks."

People making comments about whether I was fat or thin always made me cross. Seeing all the food made me cross. The way everyone was acting so desperate made me cross. Cross. Cross. *Cross*. In my previous life, I could have snapped my fingers and a similar feast would have arrived in a flash. Okay. So I hadn't eaten much for a few weeks, but I wasn't going to crack that easily!

"No. You knock it off. And if *you* call me *brat* princess once more," I said as I took a step towards her and squared up to her, "I'll show you *just* how bratty and how princessy I can be!"

"Now then, girls," warned Mario.

But Marilyn and I weren't listening. We stood opposite each other.

"Oh god," said Lynn. "Eye fight. Eye fight."

"Don't do it, Marilyn," Jake pleaded. "She could really ruin things."

"Yeah," begged Lynn. "Just leave it."

But Marilyn's eyes didn't leave mine.

And my eyes didn't leave hers.

We were in eye lock. Single combat. No weapons required.

This I can do, I thought as I stared back at her. Never mind calling me a princess, when it comes to staring an opponent down, I was queen – champion of all my previous schools. I could make my eyes go out of focus so that the person I was looking at went blurry. They couldn't tell by looking at me, but it meant that I didn't get intimidated by the other person's stare. It had worked every time apart from with Mario, but he was in a league of his own.

Seconds went by…

Minutes…

The only sound was the fire crackling in the grate. And seven people breathing.

Then finally Marilyn blinked.

"*Brrrrat*… Pr…in…cess," she said *very* slowly, almost spitting her words.

I nodded smugly. "Your choice." I turned to Mario.

"Noooooooooo," cried Jake and Lynn in unison. "Please Leonora. Think of all that lovely food. Please."

"Nooooooooooooooooooooooo," cried Marilyn. "Please, Leonora. Don't mess it up for the rest of us. Please. I didn't mean it."

"Too late," I said.

"N… n… nooooooooooooooooooo,' cried Mark, and all eyes turned to him in amazement.

"You *spoke!*" Jake exclaimed.

I wasn't moved. It took more than a chicken pie and vanilla slice to break me. "Stone circle, please, Mario. And you can tell that fat deli man he may as well put the supper back in the van."

I heard a collective gasp and a sob from Jake.

Mario nodded. "Follow me," he said. "You have until five o'clock to change your mind. And bear in mind that you will not only be ruining Christmas Eve for yourself, but also for your fellow guests." He shook his head sadly. "You just don't get being a team player do you? It's still me, me, me in your world. Where does it get you, huh?"

"Suits me," I said, and I pointed at Marilyn. "*She* asked for it."

I took one last look at the feast then walked out after Mario like a condemned prisoner going to the gallows.

Marilyn, Mark, Jake and Lynn stood to one side, their heads bowed.

"Brat Princess walking," said Jake as I went past him. "Stand back. Let her through."

Chapter Eleven

Christmas past

I sat in my stone circle in the hallway. I stared at the wood-panelled walls. I stared at the high ceiling. The paint up there was dingy with age. There was a cobweb in one corner. The only sounds were the ticking of the antique clock on the wall and the occasional gust of wind outside that rattled the windows and doors.

It was boring being there. And it was lonely.

But I wasn't giving in for anybody.

I had a doze. I rearranged the stones. I rearranged the stones again. *So much for Mars moving into Aquarius and life getting more relaxing,* I thought. *It's so relaxing, I feel comatose.*

Over the afternoon, Mark, Jake, Lynn and Marilyn crept into the hall, one after the other, and tried to reason with me.

Lynn offered to give me her pillow on nights when I'd lost the privilege of mine.

Jake offered to help with my chores.

Even Mark came and, having recovered his voice,

had a lot to say. "Please, Leonora. Don't ruin it for the others. It's bad enough being in this miserable place on a night like this. Let's at least have a decent supper. And, speaking for myself, I've never had a feast like the one in the kitchen. And neither have the others. You've known what it's like to have the best. None of us has."

I shook my head. I couldn't back down and lose face. Not at this stage of the game.

Marilyn came and threatened me. "If you don't come out of this circle this minute and 'elp us decorate, I will cut off your arm with my penknife and beat you with the soggy end."

"Oh *très amusant* Marilyn. Is that all?" I said, then I yawned and turned away from her. "Be quiet when you go hey? I think I might have a little sleep."

Cut off my arm with her penknife. She was so pathetic. I also suspected that she put the tough accent on. She needn't threaten me or worry. None of them should. I was sure that they'd get their special supper. They hadn't done anything. It was me who was to be be excluded. A special treat for Zodiac Girl. Mario and his crew wouldn't deny the others because I was being stubborn. Not on Christmas Eve. No-one would be that mean.

I lay on the floor and curled up like a cat to try to keep warm as there was a serious draught blasting in from under the front door, and there I fell into a fitful sleep. I was awoken by four chimes from the clock down the hall. It was dark and cold and I felt cramped and uncomfortable.

For a moment, I wished that Mr O had been around a bit more. Okay, so he was a bit of a luvvie-dahling, kiss-kiss actor type but he was a lot more fun than the others and although I would never let him know it, not in a million squillion years, I recognized a kindred spirit in him. He was clearly used to being the star of the show, just as I was, which is probably why he took it so personally when I was rude to him.

As I lay there, I wondered what might have happened if I hadn't stomped on my zodiac phone and had taken more of an interest in his obscure little notes. Maybe they were coded with clues as to how to get out of here. He had said that he was my guardian so maybe he had been trying to help me in some peculiar way. *Maybe I've been playing it all wrong*, I wondered. *Hadn't Mr O said something about what you resist, persists? Maybe I shouldn't have resisted being a Zodiac Girl or a team player. Maybe I should have welcomed it and seen where it could have led.*

I sat up and rubbed my arms to try to get warm again and a couple of seconds later Dr Cronus appeared.

"And have you learned your lesson?" he asked.

"Only thing I've learned is that this floor sure is hard.

So can I get up now?"

He nodded. I took that as a sign that I could go and have supper. I couldn't wait. I was starving. I'd been dreaming about all the gorgeous food that had appeared earlier in the day, so I raced to the kitchen where I expected to find the others munching away. I prayed that they'd saved a piece of something for me.

However, the scene in the kitchen had changed since this morning. The fire had gone out. The only smell in the air was the usual one of boiled onions and bleach. And there were no more Christmas carols playing. Four teenagers sat slumped at the table under a glaring overhead light. In front of them was a large pan.

"What's that?" I asked.

"Potato soup," growled Lynn.

"Potato soup! But... but where's all the yummy food?"

Four faces turned to look accusingly at me.

"They took it back, thanks to you," said Marilyn through clenched teeth.

"No!" I gasped.

"And we had to eat this disgusting stuff that tastes like puréed flour," Jake added. "All because of you."

"You're the most selfish person we have ever met," said Mark.

"And we all *hate* you," said Lynn.

A wave of disappointment flooded through me. No

Christmas supper. Not a morsel. Not a crumb. I was going to fade away altogether if this carried on. Forget size zero. I was going to be size minus zero and a half.

Vibrations of loathing were flying through the air towards me, so real I could almost see them, like snakes writhing towards me, with tiny tongues poking venom in my direction. For the second time in my life, I, Queen of I Can Stare You Back, couldn't meet someone's angry gaze. I looked away then ran to the dorm, where I flung myself on my narrow bed and pulled the duvet over my head.

It wasn't *fair*. Okay. Maybe I ought to say I'm sorry to them, but I didn't think they'd really be punished for my behaviour. Not really. *Nobody understands,* I thought as I brought the back of my right hand up to my forehead à la tragic heroine. *No-one can ever understand.*

"Leonora, LeONo...r...a..." called a soft voice.

I poked my head out of the duvet to see that Dr Cronus was standing in the doorway. He looked weird. Shimmery. I looked closer and realized that he was holding a torch under his chin, which made him look like a spook. Poppy and I used to do that to scare each other under the bed sheets on Halloween, then we'd tell ghost stories.

Hah! I thought. *New tactic. So now they're going to try to scare me into submission.* "Cut the bogeyman act, Doc. I'm not falling for it."

Dr Cronus sighed then turned off the torch. "Worth a try," he said. He beckoned me to follow him out the door.

"Why out the door?" I asked. "Why not fly right out the window like in Peter Pan and Wendy, eh? Come on, Crustyboots. Show me what you got."

Dr Cronus sighed again. "I do *so* hate you spoilt brats. I always get assigned you lot. It's because I'm the Great Taskmaster you know. He who teaches life's important lessons and it does get oh so tiresome sometimes when people resist, which they always do in the beginning. Some days I wish I could be one of the others. Like Joe. He's Jupiter you know. Everybody loves him. Or Hermie. He's my grandson and very popular."

"Oh, drop the poor-me act. If you don't like what you're doing, get lost. I never asked you to teach me lessons or whatever."

"I have no choice," said the doctor. "You are Zodiac Girl so I can't get lost no matter how much I want to. You have been chosen and I must do what I have been bidden. So get up."

"Or else?"

Mr O suddenly appeared behind him. "Or else the others won't get their Christmas breakfast or dinner either," he said.

"Christmas breakfast? There's to be a Christmas

breakfast? And a Christmas dinner?"

"Well, that all depends on you, Leonora," said Mr O. "You have been one of the most resistant Zodiac Girls we have ever had and now, enough's enough. It was up to you what you did with your month here and so far, quite frankly, it's been a waste of everyone's time. But it needn't be if you'll just let us in a little. You have so much going for you if you would just let down the wall you've put up to push the world away. Okay, so yes, Leos can want their own way, yes they can be stubborn. But they can also be strong and generous and affectionate and the best of fun. Why not be the best you can be instead of always choosing to be the worst?"

I was about to say something cheeky back but there was some truth in what Mr O had said. I knew that I was demanding and I did always push people away and where had it got me? This miserable lodge on Christmas Eve and everyone here hated me.

"Let us help you," said Mr O, "and your time here needn't be so bad."

I nodded. "Okay. Lead the way," I said with a sigh. Mr O smiled at me then left me alone with the doctor, who beckoned me to follow him out of the dorm and down through the maze of corridors until we got to a staircase at the back of the lodge. It led down to another floor that I hadn't noticed before.

"What's down there?" I asked.

"Come with me and you'll see."

The staircase had dark wooden banisters and went down one flight to a door that was carved with intricate figures. On closer inspection, I made out the twelve signs of the zodiac.

"A zodiac door," I said as I read the words under the carvings. "Aries the ram, Taurus the bull, Gemini the twins, Cancer the crab, Leo the lion, that's me, Virgo the virgin, Libra, scales, Scorpio the scorpion, Sagittarius the archer, Capricorn the goat, Aquarius the water bearer and Pisces the fish. Hey, this is really beautiful. Is it Indian? It looks Eastern."

Dr Cronus smiled. "It's from Atlantis. The only one like it in existence."

"Cool. Atlantis. Yeah. I think I know someone who went there on a holiday."

Dr Cronus almost laughed. "I very much doubt that. Atlantis is an ancient civilization."

"Yeah, so? Greece and Italy are ancient too. I'm not totally stupid. People go there on holiday."

Dr Cronus tutted. "I sincerely doubt that they have been to Atlantis," he said. "Not unless they can time-travel." He got out a huge brass key and opened the door. "You're very chatty all of a sudden."

"Just glad to be out of that stone circle," I said. "It was very dull."

Dr Cronus turned on a light and a room with floor-to-ceiling shelves appeared. They were weighed down with ancient-looking books, videos, DVDs. I looked at a couple of the labels. *Polarities and Elements.* Hmm. *That sounds complicated,* I thought. *The Quadrupicities. Ditto. Progressions. Transits. Synastry in Action.*

"Hey, this is like the kind of library a wizard would have. In fact, you look like a wizard."

Dr Cronus sighed. "If I had a penny for every time I had heard that. Just because I have a long white beard, it doesn't make me a wizard. And anyhow, our aim is to teach you to see the magic that there already is in the world. Not to do tricks."

"Yeah, yeah. Whatever," I said, then I remembered what Mr O had just said and smiled at Dr Cronus to show that I wasn't totally against him. "Hey, got any mags down here? Like *Teen Vogue* or *Elle*? *Tatler*?"

Dr Cronus turned and gave me a scathing look.

"I'll take that as a 'no' then. But what is this place?"

"My archive, and I suggest you go and sit down and be quiet while I find your file," said Dr Cronus. He pointed at a TV screen at the end of the room, in front of which was an old leather sofa with some of its stuffing coming out. "Go and sit down there and wait for me."

I did as I was told and made myself comfortable on the sofa. On the table in front were two sandwiches and a glass of milk.

"That's for you," he called. "Avocado and cheese."

"Hey, thanks, Doc," I said and gulped the first one back in about four bites. It was utterly yummy.

"And don't call me 'Doc'. I'm Dr Cronus to you. Ah, there it is," I heard him say and, moments later, he appeared with what looked like a DVD in his hand. He put it into the machine.

"Movie?" I asked. "We're going to watch a *movie*?"

The doctor nodded. "We use all the latest technology when we can. Now, as you know, I am also known as Saturn…"

"The Taskmaster," I said to show that I had listened to *some* of what he and Mr O had been droning on about.

Dr Cronus nodded. "Saturn rules the part of one's life in which one needs to learn lessons. In your case, in order to do this, we need to go back into your past and look at some of the fears that lie there."

I felt a shiver of panic. My past? He was beginning to spook me but… he couldn't know about my past. *Could he?* I wondered as I began to eat my second sandwich.

"Don't be scared, Leonora," said the doctor. "You can overcome your past. Your chart shows many strengths as yet untapped. Now watch the screen."

The blank screen grew light. A door appeared. A green door with a brass lion's head on it. It looked familiar. The door began to open. It *was* familiar.

A lump came into my throat and I stopped mid munch.

"How…?" I began, but no more words came as I continued to watch. It was our old house on the TV. Our house in England where we lived before Poppy died.

From the back of the house came the sound of laughter and the camera zoomed in. I felt as if I was there. Walking down the hall like I had done a hundred times when I'd lived there. The door to the living room opened and I felt as if someone had punched me in the stomach, for there was Poppy, her face lit up with laughter.

"How? *Where* did you get this?" I asked. I had never seen it before. I knew that there were videos and DVDs of Poppy, but I thought that I had seen them all. Knew each one frame by frame. I'd memorized every second of each of them for they were all that I had left of her.

Dr Cronus sat on a chair to my left and put a finger up to his lips to indicate that I should be quiet. "Just watch."

Poppy was sitting by the fire and cutting out patterns from a sheet of green paper in front of her.

"Leaves," I said. "She's making leaves for decorations."

For a few seconds my questions fell away. I didn't

care how Dr Cronus had got the DVD or why. I could see Poppy. My little sister at Christmas.

She was two years younger than I, with blonde hair and pretty in a delicate way, with eyes that were almost too big for her face and gave her a look of constant surprise at the world. She was never completely well and was thin and pale as far back as I could remember. She suffered from asthma attacks which would come on out of the blue and were frightening to witness as she struggled to breathe with aid of her inhaler. She had the wretched thing near her, on the table. I couldn't help but notice.

Not that she ever complained, I thought as I watched the screen. *She was always positive and generous to a fault. She'd always fetch anything I wanted just so that she could be with me. And she loved to play hairdressers and would brush my hair for ages and not complain if I squirmed my way out of returning the favour. I did love her. I did. In my own way. If I'd have known what was going to happen, of course I'd have let her know just how much a lot more often.*

"What are you thinking about, Leonora?" asked Dr Cronus as the image of her lingered for a moment. Then the screen went blank.

"Nothing," I replied as I fingered the locket around my neck. "Just plotting my revenge on my parents and how I'm going to get the press to come here and close this place down for cruelty to children."

"Is that right?" asked Dr Cronus. He looked disappointed. "Fine. You do that then. First of all though, I have a task for you."

"Okay no, not more washing up…"

"Come with me," said Dr Cronus, and he went over and pushed on one of the bookshelves. It opened up to what looked like a secret room behind.

"Cool," I said. "A false door. Is it a way out?"

"Yes and no," said the doctor as he beckoned me to go through. "It could be a way out for you if you complete the task."

I sighed. "How did I know you were going to say something like that?"

I went into the small room. It had no window and was more like a large cupboard. On the right side was an enormous pile of toys. They were of every variety: dolls, robots, soft toys, cars, planes, trains, games. Next to the toys were boxes which on closer inspection contained bath sets, books, CDs, DVDs, handkerchiefs, scarves, gloves, perfumes…

"What is this?" I asked. "A collection for the jumble?"

"Certainly not," huffed Dr Cronus. "It's all brand-new. And it's your next task. Not washing up. Wrapping up."

"Wrapping up?"

Dr Cronus nodded and pointed to a table on the left of the room where there were rolls and rolls of paper, ribbons, necklaces of tinsel, scissors, glue, sticky tape. "You can come out when you've finished," he said. "These are gifts for people who are going to be in the local hospital over Christmas. Old and young. It is time for you to take some sort of positive action. You must if you are to overcome your past and move forwards."

"Do something positive?"

"You heard me."

I looked at the mounds of presents. "*All* of them? You expect me to wrap *all* of them?"

"All of them. Leos can be very creative if they want to be, fabulously flamboyant in fact. It's time you got back in touch with the more giving side of your nature. And have a think over things while you're at it. I'm going to leave you now. There's some juice in a carton behind the door and a buzzer to the right of it. You can press it when you've finished." He gave me a totally false smile, then left the room and shut the door behind him.

I got up and tried the door. Locked. I glanced around the room. There was definitely no escape.

I sat on the floor and stared at the pile of presents for a few minutes. *I could break them*, I thought. *Rip the dolls' heads off, pull their arms off and wrap them around the teddy bear's neck. I could empty all the bath gel over the walls. Stomp on the toy trains and cars until they were nothing but splinters. Break everything! That would show old Cronie Baby what he could do with his precious lessons.* I considered the plan for a few moments. The old me would have started in an instant and created havoc, but I found myself hesitating. There was no point. I knew my captors well enough by now to know that if I didn't co-operate, they'd only find some other miserable task for me to do. And it was pointless having a tantrum as they'd take no notice or leave me in here for even longer.

I took a deep breath and picked up the first present. *I may as well get started*, I thought. *Just do the job and get it over with. Sooner done, the sooner I get out of here.*

I began wrapping, using the most basic paper and continued doing each present as fast as I could with no fancy trimmings. As I worked, my mind drifted back to Christmases gone by when Poppy had been alive and she and I would sit together and wrap up all the pressies. She delighted in every aspect of Christmas – making handmade cards with glitter and stars, decorating the tree with baked gingerbread, leaving out a beer and mince pie for Santa, apples for his reindeer, then opening her presents on the morning of December 25th. Her enthusiasm had been infectious and I'd loved the season and all that went with it – the carol services, the shopping, the yummy scrummy dinner with family and friends.

As I continued wrapping, I remembered how I loved to buy presents for everyone, then wrap them in my own special way. Mummy said I had a gift for wrapping, an artist's touch. My presents always looked the best and hardly cost anything. It didn't take much. I liked to use what I could from the garden. In December, there was always holly and ivy to pick. I used to weave the green leaves and red berries with bits of twigs that I'd spray gold then put it all together with green ribbon. I was such a different person back then. I'd even write my own plays about princes and princesses and fairies in far-off lands. Poppy used to watch me perform them with her enormous brown eyes and I'd feel like I was making magic in front of her.

And now I'm here in a cupboard on my own on Christmas Eve and everybody hates me. And I am so-ooooo sa-aaaaadddddddd. Probably the loneliest person in the whole world. A tidal wave of self-pity flooded through me. Tears came to my eyes. *Poor, poor me. All by myself.* I looked around at the gifts waiting to be wrapped. *And poor them. Those people in hospital. Among strangers. These gifts are to make them feel better — how could I have thought about ruining them, even for a second?! That would have been so mean of me when they were having a tough time anyway, away from home and family and friends… like me.* I looked at the untouched ribbon and tinsels and bows on the table. *I will wrap these presents. And not only will I wrap them, but I'll wrap them really, really beautifully as well, so that the faces of the sick people will light up when they see them. That will show Old Croniebum. He won't be expecting that! Hah! He thinks he knows me, but he doesn't. Nobody does. I used to be caring once. I used to have friends! Yes. I ca-aaaa-aan b...be (sob, sob) n...ni-iiiice. N...NOBODY (sob, sob) u...understands m... m... meeeeeeeeee.*

After a good cry, I set about my task with renewed enthusiasm and found that my old talent for making gifts look special soon came back. To get myself even more in the mood, I sang Christmas carols at the top of my voice. Minutes went by as I tied and glued and cut and pasted. Hours. I lost track of time as I beavered on and the pile of unwrapped presents decreased.

When I'd finished wrapping all the gifts, I didn't press the buzzer to let Dr Cronus know. Instead I set about perfecting the finishing touches. Then tweaking and adding bits and pieces until every gift looked totally unique, a work of art with paper flowers and leaves and bows and twirls of coloured ribbon and tape. The posh present wrapper in the swankiest store in Paris couldn't have done a better job.

As I was twirling a length of silver ribbon into a double bow, the door opened and Dr Cronus put his head around. He looked at the pile of gifts stacked neatly to the left of the room. "Wow!" he said.

"Good, aren't they?" I said with a smile.

He walked in and examined a couple of the boxes on top. "No. Not good. They're blooming *astonishing*." He turned and looked at me. "Look what you're capable of. Just look! What happened, Leonora? What happened to make you so angry with the world?" He was looking at me with such kindness in his eyes that for a moment, I forgot he was one of my captors. I felt a fresh wave of sadness rushing up to the surface.

"You can tell me, Leonora," the doctor urged. "Let it out…"

"I… I… Poppy died. Our house over here was sold soon after," I said. "Too many memories, Mum and Dad said. We moved to the Caribbean but nothing was the same again. Life for me lost its colour. And so did Christmas." I sighed and I was *almost* in tears again but then I remembered that Cronus *wasn't* my friend and I had made a vow not to ever let any of them see me cry. I shook the sad feelings away and made myself put my inner wall back up. "But that was then and this is now."

"You had a happy home," said the doctor. "A happy life. And now I am going to let you in on a great secret, one of life's greatest lessons and if you can learn it, your time on this earth will be marvellous. It needn't be over just because life dealt you some difficult cards. Life is what *you* make it. Just like making a movie. In fact, you write, you direct and you act in *your* own movie. The movie of your life. Never forget that. You still have a say in it all. Okay, one of the characters has gone. Your sister, Poppy. But you're still here. But what part are you playing now? Do you *like* the character you have written for yourself? This Brat Princess that the others call you? Do you like your script? The dialogue that you have given to yourself? If you were watching yourself now on a screen, would you be proud of your part?"

"Oh god, not more psychobabble," I groaned. "Pul-*leese*."

Dr Cronus let out one of his sighs. "I repeat. You are the writer, the director and the actor in your own play," he said. "It is always up to you what you make of it, just as it is up to you what you make of your month as Zodiac Girl. And now you can go and join the others. I think they may be having a carol session as, don't forget, it's Christmas."

I got up and left the room. *Okay.* I thought. *I write my own character? So? Yeah. I'm Leonora Hedley-Dent. Rich girl. Pretty great part if you ask me. I have a life that people envy when I'm not stuck in this awful place. I do... don't I?* But seeing the footage of Poppy then remembering my Christmases gone by had made me think. I felt strange, like some of the anger had gone out of me and had been replaced by an overwhelming sense of sadness. I didn't know which was worse. Anger or sadness. When I was angry at least I could blame everyone else. But this new feeling. This emptiness. I didn't know what to do with it. Who to direct it at.

Christmas, I said to myself. *Hah blooming bumbag!*

Chapter Twelve

Christmas present

"We don't want her with us," said Jake as I came out of the front door to find the others from the lodge hunched around a camp fire with Mr O, Miss Lunie Petunie and Mario. Although I didn't show it, I was pleased to see that Mr O was still around. He seemed back to his sunny self and was busy toasting marshmallows. The others were each wearing a pair of reindeer's antlers, an anorak and a gloomy expression. If I hadn't felt so miserable, I might have laughed.

"And I don't want to be here," I said, "but Cronie Baby says that there might be a Christmas breakfast for you lot if I co-operate. So what's going on out here?"

"As a special treat, hah, pardon me while I laugh," droned Marilyn, "Mario made us build this fire so that we could sit around and sing Christmas carols."

Selene got up and handed me a pair of felt antlers. I was about to object, then remembered that I had to co-operate or no posh nosh tomorrow. I took them, put them on and sat at the edge of the circle. *My Prat of the Year look is now complete,* I thought. *Curly hair, brown eyes, navy trackies and now antlers. And to think that, only a few weeks ago, I was Queen of Style.*

I looked around the camp fire. Marilyn, Lynn, Jake and Mark's faces were pink from the glow of the fire. Each of them looked far away, probably lost in their memories of Christmases gone by as well. The atmosphere felt sad. Even Mark's usual scowl had been replaced by a look of regret.

How has it come to this? I asked myself. I never in a million thousand trillion billion years thought that, at the age of fourteen, I'd be apart from Mummy and Daddy on Christmas Eve of all nights. I rubbed Poppy's locket between my finger and thumb again, needing to know that it was there. It had been hers. She had been wearing it on the day she died. The nurses gave it to us in a transparent plastic bag along with her Little Mermaid watch, her blue bead bracelet and her inhaler. I'd put the locket on and hadn't taken it off since that day. Not once. Not even in the bath. At the thought of that little bag of her belongings, I felt tears spill out of my eyes and down my cheeks. I quickly brushed them away before anyone saw. *If only,* I thought. *If only I'd behaved differently that day. If only. If only. If only I could turn back time and make it right I would because her death was all my fault. I am such a bad person. And I will never forgive myself, ever.*

I glanced around again. One more week to go. And deck the halls with Christmas holly, tra la la la la, la la la laaaaaah.

As we sat staring into the embers of the fire and chewing on the marshmallows that Mr O handed round, there was the familiar roar of Hermie's bike and indeed, a few moments later, he appeared and skidded to a halt in front of the fire. Even he had made an effort for Christmas and his usual garb of black leather was adorned with garlands of tinsels. He reached into the box on the back of his bike and pulled out five packages. "I bring greetings from the outside world," he said as he chucked them over to us. "Jake, Marilyn, Lynn, Mark and… yep, one for you, Leonora."

Everyone was silent as they ripped off the paper.

Mark's parcel contained a video phone. Jake got a card and a Terry's Chocolate Orange which he immediately opened and passed round. It tasted like heaven. Lynn got a pink woolly scarf, which she wrapped round her neck. And Marilyn got a card with a photo and a bunch of music CDs.

"What have you got?" asked Lynn.

I looked down at the box on my knee. It was a portable DVD player. And a DVD.

Hermie pointed at a switch. "That's the on button," he said.

"I know," I said.

"What is it?" asked Jake. "A Christmas movie to pass the time? Can we all watch?"

"It's a message from your mum and dad," Hermie said.

I sat and looked at the DVD player. It felt like it was a bomb waiting to go off. *What if the DVD was a movie with Poppy in it and the others asked me about her?* I wondered. *What would I say?* I was about to put it in my pocket when Mr O shook his head.

"I think we should all share what we've received tonight," he said. "In the spirit of Christmas, I'd like to hear what you've got and what it means to you."

There was a collective groan. "Noooooooooo."

Mr O clapped his hands. "Okay, then let's play a game first. Role reversal."

There was another collective groan. "Nooooooooo."

Mr O took no notice of any of us. "Okay. Who shall we have go first?"

"Leonora," said Marilyn. "It's only fair seeing as she messed supper up for us."

I knew I had to co-operate. If I didn't there would be no breakfast. Plus, I was starting to tire of being so objectionable *all* the time. I'd show them. I *could* play nice. "Okay. Who do you want me to be?"

Mr O beamed and gave me the thumbs up. "You can play your mother," he said. "And... Marilyn, you can be Leonora."

Marilyn leapt up. "Love to." She immediately put a really sour expression on her face.

"I don't do that," I said.

"You soooo do," chorused Lynn, Jake and Mark.

Marilyn started flouncing about like a total drama queen. "I am so superior. I don't know whaaaat I am doing here with these losers. Oh loser," she turned to Selene, "get me a toastie would you? And make it snappy." Then she turned to Mark. "And slave boy, get me a goose-down duvet would you. I am sooooo cold. Brrr. Never mind the others? Who cares about them? Oh me me me me me me me. Oh my hair! It's gone curly. Oh. I think I might die. And that shampoo? It's like sooooooo last century."

The others cracked up laughing. Not me, though. I felt *outraged.*

"Go on, Leonora," urged Mr O. "Be your mum. You can do it."

I felt like my legs had turned to concrete, but I forced myself to move. *You can do this,* I told myself. *If there's one thing I can do better than anything, that's act. My life since Poppy died has all been an act.* "Now then sweetheart…" I began as I got up.

Marilyn turned and gave me a scathing look. "I'm not your sweetheart. I'm nobody's sweetheart, and I'll be suing your sorry butt as soon as I get out of here."

Jake fell on the floor laughing.

"But it's for your own good, dear," I said in Mummy's gentle voice and even if I say it myself, I had it down rather well. Drama was my best subject at school, even before accounting. I glanced over at Mr O and he gave me an encouraging wink.

Marilyn folded her arms and pinched her mouth in. "You're not my mother. I disown you. I *hate* you."

It was so weird because when she said that she hated me, it hurt. "No darling, please don't…"

"Oh don't simper, Mummy. You're like… so… *annoying*. Like pardon you for squeaking," snapped Marilyn as she stepped forward and gave me a good shove, so forceful that I fell back into a bush. That hurt too, and as I lay there, I realised that pushing someone into a bush was exactly what I had done to Daddy on the day I left to board the plane just three weeks previously.

"Okay, well done girls," said Selene. "Yes. Er. Enough now. Come on, Leonora. Up you come." She got up and came over to where I lay and offered her hand.

"Just give me a mo," I said. "Please." I lay in the bush and closed my eyes. A hundred tantrums I'd had in the past year flashed through my mind. The hurtful words I had said to Mummy and Daddy. The moods. The slammed doors. Phone calls cut short. I opened my eyes to see Marilyn still flouncing around being Brat

Princess à la Leonora Hedley-Dent and I thought about what old Cronus had just said about life being like a movie. Well, if that was true, I might have the lead role in my personal film but my character stank. *She needs a major rewrite*, I thought as I pulled a twig out of my hair then continued looking up at the black sky. *I have been the daughter from hell. No wonder Mummy and Daddy sent me here.*

A few moments later, I scrambled out of the bush and Mr O patted the ground beside him to indicate that I should go and sit by him.

"Okay?" he asked as I took my place.

I nodded, but I felt peculiar – as if I was waking from a long, stressful dream.

We played out some more scenarios. Lynn got to be Dr Cronus, which she did very well – grumping and scowling her way around the camp fire and threatening us all with extra lessons. Mark got to be Selene, and he played her as a madwoman who lived her life by the phases of the Moon and who liked to do strange dances to "get her feelings out." Mark was turning out to be good fun since he'd started talking, and Selene took his impersonation like a great sport and laughed along with the rest of us.

When the role-playing had finished, Selene asked to see what we had all got in our packages.

"You go first, Jake," he said.

Jake held up sticky fingers. "Chocolate. It's my

favourite. Mum always gets it for me at Christmas." He showed us the card that accompanied the chocolate. Inside it was a photo of a boy who looked like a younger version of Jake. He had a sweet face and was in a hospital bed. His parents were on either side and the boy was holding up a teddy bear with a Christmas hat on. It made me think of all the times that my family had accompanied Poppy to the hospital when she couldn't breathe and that last fateful time when she didn't come home with us. I glanced at Jake's earnest face and hoped that he never had to go through the same.

"What's the matter with your brother?" I asked.

Jake shrugged. "Some kind of autoimmune disease I think it's called."

"Can they help him?"

Jake shook his head. "Not here they can't. They could if we sent him to America. There's a man there who could help him but we can't afford it."

"Is that why you stole cars?" asked Selene.

Jake nodded. "Yeah. Partly. I was trying to raise the money. But... I enjoyed it too. It was a laugh. Some'at to do to take my mind off things."

Mario got up and stood threateningly over Jake. "But you won't be doing that kind of thing any more *will* you?"

Jake coughed. "Er, no. Course not, sir."

"Good," said Mario. "Because, if you do, you'll be

back here before you can say BMW. Your choice. So who's next? Mark?"

Mark showed us his video phone. His family had recorded a message for him and he showed us a busy family scene, with dogs, cats, babies, grandparents, parents, siblings. All the adults were singing "We Wish You a Merry Christmas". They looked like fun.

"They must have clubbed together to get it for me," said Mark. "I would have nicked it from somewhere if I'd been home probably." Then he coughed and glanced at Mario. "But not any more, sir. No, sir. I have mended my ways. Sir."

We all laughed.

"Sounds like your family knows how to enjoy Christmas," said Selene.

Mark nodded. "Yeah. I guess so. Might be the last one in that house though. Come the New Year, they're going to be evicted. The landlord put up the rent. My dad lost his job. My mum has done everything she can, but no joy. My family will be homeless."

"Maybe something will turn up," said Selene. "You never know what's around the next corner."

"Yes, I do. Homelessness," snapped Mark, and he punched his right palm with his left hand. "And there's *nothing* I can do about it. Not in here where the stupid social services sent me."

Oh god, here we go with the sob stories again, I thought

when I noticed that Mr O was giving me a very pointed look.

"What?" I asked.

"And what do you think of Mark's situation?" he asked.

I shrugged. "Yeah. Tough. Win some, lose some."

Mr O looked at me with narrowed eyes, then sighed heavily. Whatever he was thinking, it wasn't happy thoughts.

"What did you get, Lynn?" asked Selene.

"A scarf from Mum. She wouldn't send a photo. Not of her and *him*. She knows how I feel about my stepfather, but…"

"And how do you feel about him?" Selene asked.

Lynn shifted about, then stared at her feet. "I guess… well, sometimes people deserve a second chance don't they?"

When she said that, we all knew that she was talking about herself and not just her mum or her stepfather. And then I noticed that Mr O was giving me his pointed look again.

"What? *What?*" I asked.

Mr O just pouted by way of reply. *He's such a drama queen,* I thought. "I'm not psychic," I said. "If you're trying to tell me something just tell me."

"Hah!" said Mr O. "*Now* she wants to listen. Honestly! In all my days I have never had one like you."

"What do you mean?" I asked.

"One who ignores me like *you* do. Really. Leos can be self-centred at the best of times, but you! You take the prize. Leonora – it's *clear* what you have to do. But have you listened? Learned anything? Oh no. First you smashed your phone and then you rip up all my messages. All that good advice I've been sending you. All in the bin. Don't think I don't know."

Oops, I thought. "Oh that. Yeah. I know. Er… sorry? Um. I will try to be better. Is that what you want to hear? Is that why you're giving me those pointed looks?"

Mr O sighed heavily. "I give up," he said, then he turned to the others. "This time here could have changed everything for Leonora, but I fear she's going to blow it by being stubborn. It does happen sometimes. Not often. Most girls are over the moon to be a Zodiac Girl. Okay sometimes it takes some adjusting to, but never, *never* before have I had one who rejects the whole idea *and* breaks her phone."

"Oo er," I said. "Listen to you, lord of the luvvies. Just because you're not the centre of attention you don't like it. Honestly, the way you go on, you really do think everything revolves around you, don't you?"

There was an awkward silence, then Selene coughed. "Well, it does actually… he *is* the Sun."

"Okay," said Mark. "Enough. What is all this?

Maybe someone could explain. This zodiac thing? Even that deli guy who was here with the food was on about it. He called you a Zodiac Girl, Leonora. What's it all about exactly?"

"Every month, somewhere on the planet, a girl is chosen to be a Zodiac Girl…" Selene began. I glanced at Mr O. He seemed to have gone into a major sulk which made me want to smile. I was beginning to feel very fond of him. He could stick his bottom lip out further than I could.

"Chosen how?" asked Lynn.

"Different elements every time," Selene continued. "The only thing that each Zodiac Girl has in common is that it happens at a turning point in her life and for one month, she gets the aid of the planets."

I sighed. I knew there was no keeping the fact that I was this month's Zodiac Girl hush-hush any longer. "Blah blah de blah. Oh come on, surely I'm not the only one who has heard them going on about the Moon and the stars and Mr O saying he is the Sun."

"Yeah, but I thought he was speaking metaphorically," said Marilyn. "You know, like 'e's a little ray of sunshine and that."

I shook my head. "Nope. He thinks he *is* the Sun. As in the planet. Don't you, Mr O?"

Mr O stuck his bottom lip out even further while Jake burst out laughing. "No way," he said.

"Yeah. No way. You're saying to me that Mr O said that he was the manifestation of the Sun?" asked Lynn. "Do you think that, Mr O? Do you?"

"I'm not saying anything," said Mr O, "in fact, I may not stay around if I'm not going to be appreciated."

He got up and flounced off into the dark garden. Mario, Selene and Hermie rushed after him and we could hear them reasoning with him a distance away. I could just about make out, "She's not going to change." "Some you just have to accept are stuck in their ways..."

"It's not just him," I continued. "Lunie Petunie thinks she's the Moon, Dr Cronus thinks he's Saturn, Mario is Mars and Hermie is apparently none other than Mercury, the planet of communication here in earthly form as a motorbike messenger boy."

Marilyn rolled her eyes to the sky. "Pff. Yeah, right."

"Are you winding us up?" asked Mark.

I shook my head. "Honest. That's what they think."

Lynn looked troubled. "Oh. My. God. I thought there was something different about them, but I thought that it was you, me, Mark, Lynn and Marilyn who were supposed to need help."

"I know. Do you think that our parents know that they signed us away to a bunch of crazies?" asked Marilyn.

"Probably not," said Lynn. "But... how come no-one's mentioned any of this zodiac stuff to the rest of us. Only to you."

"Not just me. Dr Cronus goes on about it just about every day in classes," I said.

"Yeah, I guess... but I thought that was just a lesson in astronomy and no-one listens to 'im much anyway and 'e didn't say much about you being a Zodiac Girl," said Marilyn as behind her Mr O, Mario, Selene and Hermie returned to the fire.

Jake leaned over and whispered, "If what Leonora is saying is true or even half true, best play along – not let on that we know they need locking up right?"

Mark, Marilyn and Lynn quickly nodded and assumed their usual blank expressions.

"It's all true!" boomed Mr O. "We are the planets and Leonora is Zodiac Girl. Every case is different depending on the needs of the girl in question, but never before has someone so ruthlessly rejected our help!"

"Okay. So what does Leonora need then?" asked Jake. "Maybe we can help."

Mr O glared at him for a second as if doubting his sincerity, but then he sat down cross-legged by the fire. "Only she can discover that," he said. "I was only here to guide and advise. But if she won't listen what can I do?"

"I'll listen," I said. If listening meant breakfast, I

could do that easy-peasy plus I had genuinely grown to like Mr O, mad or not. "And I'm sorry if I've been rude. Yeah. I am. Really."

Mr O looked at me very closely as if trying to gauge if I was being sincere. I looked back at him and smiled.

He looked taken aback, but smiled in return. "Hmm," he said.

"So please, what's next on my zodiac agenda?" I asked.

"Neptune," he said.

"Neptune. That's a new one. I don't think you've mentioned that before," I said doing my best to look as enthusiastic as I could.

Mr O still looked a little suspicious.

"So what's Neptune all about then?' I asked.

"You really want to know?"

I nodded.

"Mystery," said Mr O. "Illusion. Neptune governs the realm where nothing is quite what it seems. The realm of dreams, in fact."

"Can't wait," I said. "And when will I get to meet him or is it a her?"

"Him," said Mr O. "Tonight. Neptune is in conjunction with Pluto at an angle to—"

"Two of them. A double whammy," Lynn interrupted. "Lucky you, Leonora."

"So what's Pluto about?" asked Marilyn with a sly

wink at me. I winked back. Mario Mars couldn't accuse me of not being a team player now. We were backing each other up brilliantly.

"Pluto is the planet of transformation," said Mr O.

"Impressive," said Jake.

"He is," said Selene. "Depending on where Pluto is in your birth chart, can mean matters of life or death."

"Life or death huh?" said Lynn. "Sounds ser…ious." She almost blew it on the last line by laughing but checked herself just in time.

"So are these guys coming to the lodge then?" I asked.

"It is up to them how or when they choose to make themselves known to you," said Mr O.

"Sounds spooky," said Marilyn. "You just give us a shout if you need a hand, Leonora."

I felt touched by her offer to help. It was the kindest gesture she'd made since I had arrived at the lodge. "What did you get in your package?" I asked, and put on my best "I am really interested" look. Mr O continued staring at me, so I turned and winked at him. He looked more confused than ever.

Marilyn showed us the photo of her mum. She was about forty, with short dark hair and a kind but sad face. Marilyn looked wistful as she showed it, and I wondered if she was regretting how she'd behaved towards her mum in the past, just as I was beginning to regret the way I'd acted with my parents.

And then it was my turn. I so hoped that Mum or Dad didn't say anything that gave anything away. Poppy was my secret and, even after all that had happened, I wasn't ready to share her with the group. They hated me enough as it was. They'd only hate me more when they found out what I'd done. I took a deep breath and turned on the DVD player.

Mummy and Daddy's image filled the seven-inch frame.

Mummy looked tearful, then she also took a deep breath and began to speak. "Darling Leo. We've only been given a minute to talk to you on here so I'll make it quick. I just wanted to say that I love you very much. And I always will."

Next to her, Daddy nodded.

"We regret that we had to take such severe measures," Mummy continued, "but felt we had no option. None of us could go on as we were."

"And, Leonora," Daddy interrupted, "we want you to know that we don't blame you. We never have. It wasn't your fault and you mustn't blame yourself. We love you now and we have always have and—"

"—we hope to see you very soon," Mummy finished for him.

For a few seconds, it felt like I was home, where I belonged, but then the screen went fuzzy then black and

I was back around a camp fire with a bunch of strangers outside a lodge in the middle of the moors on Christmas Eve on a cold, cold night. The sense of belonging that I had felt earlier faded away like warm breath in the air on a freezing night and I made myself put my inner wall back up stronger than ever.

And then the inevitable questions came.

"What mustn't you blame yourself for?" asked Lynn.

"What did you do?" asked Mark.

"What don't they blame you for?" asked Jake.

"Nothing. For being a pain probably," I said. It was a half-truth. I couldn't tell the whole story. No-one knew that. Not even Mummy and Daddy. And no-one would ever understand. *Mummy and Daddy can say that they don't blame me,* I thought as the fire grew dim and the others grew sleepy, *but they don't know what really happened on the day that Poppy died. Only I know that and I can never forgive myself.*

When I got back to the dorm, I wrote another letter.

Dear Mummy and Daddy

I am miserable. Please let me out. Everyone hates me. I hate myself. I know I am bad, but I will try to change. I am sorry about everything.

Yours,

Leonora

Chapter Thirteen
Christmas future

I was in a hospital room. There was an empty bed. A man and a woman were putting clothes and bits and pieces into a suitcase. Where was I? In the hospital where Poppy was? No. It wasn't there, although the man and woman looked familiar. Not my mum and dad, though. No. It was *Jake's* mum and dad. What was I doing watching them? How did I get there? And where was his younger brother?

A man with a white beard and what appeared to be a broom walked in. "You're dreaming," he said, and his broom turned into a trident, like the one that you see the king of the sea carrying. Least you do on the bags that Mummy used to get our fish and chips in when we lived in England in our country house. The shop she used was called Poseidon. I think he was the king of the sea. It was then that I remembered why the village of Osbury had seemed familiar when we had driven through it on the way up to the lodge. *Of course. That's it!* I thought as it came back to me. It was where

Mum used to go to do her shopping and get her hair done. I *knew* I had been there before.

"Who are you?" I asked.

"The planet Neptune," he said.

"Ah yes. I was told to expect you. You rule the realm of dreams, yeah?"

The old man nodded.

"Cool. I've met some of your mates already," I continued. "So where's Jake's brother then?"

Neptune shook his head. "He didn't make it."

"What do you mean didn't make it?" I gasped.

Neptune acted out someone's throat being cut.

"You mean kaput?" I asked.

He nodded and disappeared then a moment later, another figure appeared. He looked like a handsome goth prince. Younger than the king of the sea. He was tall, dressed in black with a pale long face and hair tied back in a ponytail. He bowed. "Leonora. At your service. I'm PJ."

"Pluto?"

"Indeed. Some call me PJ, but I am also known as Pluto, ze great renewer."

"Excellent. And I'm dreaming apparently. Is that why Jake's parents haven't noticed me?"

PJ nodded. "Zey can't see you."

"So why are you here?"

"I've been sent to help wiz your transformation.

159

To show you a few things."

"Like what?" I said. I was enjoying the encounter with him and Neptune. I felt as if I was floating and everything was unreal.

"Like your future."

"Oh. Okay. But what about Jake's brother? Is what happens to him part of my future?"

"Zat depends on you."

That made me feel confused and I tried to make myself wake up, but it didn't seem to be happening. PJ beckoned for me to follow him out of the room.

It was weird. I walked out through the door, but instead of finding a hospital corridor we were out in a small room in what appeared to be a shabby hotel. I could see through a grimy window that it was raining outside. In a room of the hotel there was a family eating a takeaway pizza. They also looked familiar. I soon recognized them. They were Mark's family, complete with cat, but they didn't look as happy as they had on Mark's video phone. Even the cat looked fed up. A middle-aged lady looked like she had been crying and the man with her who I presumed was Mark's dad looked like he had the weight of the world on his shoulders. It made me feel sad just looking at them. *It's a dream, a dream,* I told myself, although it was beginning to feel more like a *bad* dream. *Not my responsibility. Thank God my family at least has a home, several in fact, and food and lots of money.*

"Hey, PJ, my man," I said. "Charming though you are, why are you showing me the future of my fellow inmates but not what's ahead for me?"

"Look, Leonora, look again. Zeir future iz tied wiz yours."

"Yeah, right," I scoffed. "I don't think so. Me rich. They poor. I will be going home to a very nice house with staff and these people... well..."

"Homeless," said PJ in a flat voice. "Zey are in a hostel for ze homeless."

"Whatever. So what's next on the agenda? The starving people in Africa?"

PJ gave me a filthy look. As if what he'd been showing me was *my* fault. "Don't you care, Leonora?"

"Yeah. Course. But for one thing, this is a *dream*. And in real life, there are people who work to help the poor aren't there? Charities. Social workers. In case you hadn't noticed, I'm a fourteen-year-old girl. What can I do?"

"More zan most fourteen year-olds, zat's for sure," PJ scoffed, and I got a strong feeling that he didn't like me. I pulled a face at him as he beckoned me on. I was glad that Mr O was my guardian and not this intense-looking misery.

"I am so not interested. Come on, then, show me something impressive. Show me *my* future."

PJ paused for a second as if considering my request,

then he beckoned me on. "You asked for it," he said.

We left behind Mark's family, walked though the door of the hostel and found ourselves in a shop. A scruffy shop full of all sorts of things: clothes, shoes, toys, curtains, pots, pans in fact, it looked like... a charity shop! I'd never been inside of one before but had seen them from the outside. *What am I doing in here?* I wondered. It felt so peculiar. *Remember, you are dreaming,* I reminded myself as I looked around and saw...

Nooooooooooooooooo! No. No. No. No. NOOOOOOOO.

This time it wasn't the people who look familiar. It was the stuff on sale. Rails and rails of what looked like *MY* wardrobe. And my shoes! And people were pawing over it like it was on sale! *No waaaaay,* I thought. Of all the things I'd seen, this had to be the worst.

"These are *my* things!" I said as I tried to pull a pair of shoes out of a woman's hand. To no avail, my hands went right through her. And then I noticed the price on the shoes. Two pounds fifty! *Totally freaky!*

I fell to my knees. "Oh PJ please. Make this stop. Come on, this isn't a dream any more. This is a *nightmare*. Those shoes are labelled two quid. They're by Jimmy Choo and they're worth four hundred!" I tried to say, *noooo, leave my things alone* to the woman holding the shoes but she couldn't hear me. It was as if my mouth was full of a huge wad of chewing gum. It was only when I spoke to PJ that my words came out properly and he looked like he was finding the whole scene very amusing.

"Don't you vonder vhy your clozing iz here?" he asked.

"Yeah. No," I felt confused. "It's not real is it? Like not really happening? Like, a dream yeah?"

"Sometimes our dreams show uz our future," said PJ.

I felt a shiver of dread go up my spine. "And you're saying that my clothes will be on sale in some second-hand shop? No. *Never.* Mummy and Daddy would never allow it. Nooooooo. Why would they? Please. Not this. Don't show me this. Anything but this."

PJ chuckled then beckoned me into a changing room. I got up to follow him wondering what horrors awaited me in there. Some tramp in one of my "Chanel teen" range dresses? Some stinky poor person in one of my Versace tops? It was too *too* horrible. But no. PJ and I were in a church. There was the sound of a choir. A few people in pews. In the centre was a coffin covered with white roses.

These people were the most familiar of all. In the front pew were Mummy and Daddy. A wave of joy flooded through me.

"Mummy, Daddy," I cried but they didn't even look up.

"Zey can't hear you remember?" PJ reminded me.

And there were Shirla, Mason and Henry in the

second row. And my darling Coco, her fur back to its natural white colour.

"Oh no. PJ, please. Don't show me Poppy's funeral."

"Not Poppy's," said PJ and with a snap of his fingers, we were outside. We were in a cemetery. My parents were there again under a green umbrella that almost blew inside out in the gale. Rain lashed down, but it didn't touch me. Shirla and Henry and Mason were standing with my parents under a second huge umbrella. I looked at the gravestone. It *was* Poppy's grave. I remembered it well. The engraving of her name had been etched in my heart as well as on the stone. Beloved daughters... WAIT a minute! Beloved *daughters*? As in plural! Poppy Hedley-Dent and... Leonora Hedley-DENT!!!!!! Leonora. Hedley. Dent. That was me. *That* was my grave! My name. Noooooooooo. It couldn't be. Not me. Not dead. Not six feet under! *No. No. It's a dream*, I told myself again. *Mr O warned me. Neptune. An encounter with the planet where things are not as they appear to be. And Pluto, the planet that deals with life and death.*

"Hah! They're not even crying," I said as I turned to PJ. "Surely they'd cry just a little bit? Hey. You're not Death are you?"

"Some people might say zat I am. I am Pluto and if you don't mind, I don't like ze word 'death', I prefer ze words 'mortally challenged'."

I almost laughed. "A politically correct phantom. Oh, get a life will you?"

PJ gave me a scathing look. "You may laugh, but you should listen to me. I don't just deal in death. I deal in ze transformation."

"So you keep telling me. Look mate, PJ, Pluto or whoever, I'm having a really bad dream and I'd like you to butt out of it if you don't mind. I..." I pointed at the gravestone. "That's my grave down there. Least it's not... because I'm up here, but... look here, I'd like to go back to the dorm now and wake up. For this to be over."

PJ nodded. "To dream about death doesn't necessarily mean a physical death. It can be symbolic. Like ze end of something."

"Whatever. Yeah, but *was* that really my future? Is that what's going to happen or only what *might* happen?"

"Maybe it signifies ze end of something, Leonora."

"The end of what? What?"

"Listen to vot zey are saying," urged PJ, and suddenly I could hear the people by the grave – as if someone had suddenly turned up the sound on a movie.

"None of her friends turned up," said Henry.

"What friends?" asked Shirla. "She pushed them all away. No-one stayed her friend for long."

Henry shook his head. "What a shame. What a

lonely little girl she was."

Mason scoffed. "Don't feel sorry for her. She was a total brat. A brat princess. No wonder she didn't have any friends."

"What will happen to her money?" asked Shirla. "Her savings account?"

"Her parents have become so disillusioned with money and all that goes with it that they are going to give all of their and Leonora's savings away. Her clothes have already gone to charity."

"NooooooooooooooooooooooOOOOOOOOOO," I groaned. "I HAAAATE this dream. Get me out if it!"

PJ put a finger to his lips as if to hush me.

"Least we're off the hook then," said Shirla. "We won't have to repay our loans plus the interest. Glory be for that!"

"Amen," said Henry. "Amen."

"I still feel sorry for her a bit," said Shirla. "I think she never did get over the death of her sister."

"It's true," said Mason. "She was a sweet kid before that."

"I find that hard to believe," said Henry. "But that was before my time. What happened?"

Shirla shook her head as if even to think about it was hard.

"Her younger sister," she said. "She had an asthma attack. Leonora, she blame herself although it wasn't her fault. Poor Poppy. Some nasty kid at their school had been picking on her... a bully..."

I nodded. "Mo Bolton," I whispered.

"One night, this girl and her friends, they's taunting young Poppy on her way home. She starts to have an asthma attack and Mo runs off with the inhaler, laughing like crazy, not realizing that, without it, the poor girl couldn't breathe."

I felt tears come to my eyes. "That was my fault, *my* fault. I should have been there."

"Vhy vas it your fault, Leonora?" asked PJ. "It vasn't you who ran off wiz the inhaler. You loved Poppy."

A crippling pain hit my stomach and I buckled over. "Enough. Don't make me talk about this. Think about this. I fear *this* more than anything else. Please, let it go. Let me wake up now."

"You can tell me," said PJ. "I'm not real. It iz only a dream, remember. Only a dream, so no-one else vill ever know vot you say. It's just between you and me."

I felt my head begin to spin and was finding it hard to breathe, dream or no dream.

"I... I... can't..."

"Leonora, talk to me. You can tell me everyzing. Leonora, you must let it out."

I crumpled to my knees on the floor. Without looking at PJ's face, I began to tell him what happened that fateful night.

"We went home together after school every day. Mo Bolton didn't bother her when I was around. She wouldn't dare. I could see her off easy. But that day…" I felt a huge sob come into my throat, like a bubble stuck there blocking my speech.

"Go on, Leonora," PJ urged.

I forced myself to breathe. "… my friend Jasmine, she wanted to go to the mall and I wanted to go with her. Course Poppy wanted to come with us, but I said no."

"Why did you say no, Leonora?"

"I was… I was worried that Jasmine wasn't my friend any more. She'd been spending more and more time with another girl in our class and I… I wanted to make sure we were still bezzies."

"Bezzies?"

"Best friends. Jasmine was my best friend and one of the most popular girls in our year. I really wanted to stay in with her because it meant that I was popular too. So I told Poppy to go home on her own. It wasn't far. Our school was only at the end of our road, but… I shouldn't have let her go. She was crying and I told her to grow up and stop acting like a crybaby. Mo and her mates were hiding down an alley two houses away from the lane that led to our house."

"Had zat ever happened before, Leonora?"

I shook my head. "Mo lived on the other side of town. I don't know what she was doing down our way."

"And had Poppy ever gone home on her own before?" PJ asked.

I nodded. "Sometimes. Not often though. I usually went with her, but this night... it was as if she had an instinct that something was going to happen. Mo had threatened her during the day. We never got to find out as Mo was taken to a special school afterwards. All sorts of people came out after Poppy's death and said what a bully Mo was. But it was too late by then. Too late for my sister. I felt mean not letting her go with me, but I... I wanted to stay in with Jas. If only, if only I..." And then a dam burst inside of me. All the tears I had been holding back came flooding through like an avalanche.

PJ placed his hand on my back and let me sob my heart out to him.

"I'm so sorry. *So* sorry. Don't you see now? It was... my... fault and my last words to her were to scram. That she was... a silly crybaby. I didn't want her around. You should have seen her face. Like I'd b...b...broken her heart. That face has stayed with... me... for ever."

PJ gently stroked my hair. "You poor, poor child," he said. "Poor, poor child."

And that set me off crying again. I know I didn't

deserve anyone to be nice. Anyone to call me a poor child and stroke my hair. I was wicked. Hateful. The worst person alive.

"After Poppy's death, I thought that I would never let anyone close again, so I put a wall up. Made myself not care. I wouldn't let anyone in."

"Understandable," said PJ in a gentle voice.

PJ let me cry until there were no tears left. And nothing more to say. Just a feeling of complete and utter exhaustion. I felt like I hadn't slept for a million years. *But I was asleep, wasn't I? Wasn't I? It was all a dream.*

"Am I still dreaming?" I asked.

"Look around you," said PJ and, when I did so, I saw that I was in the dorm, back in my narrow bed at the lodge. I opened my eyes and sat up. PJ was sitting on the end of the bed. From the end of the room came the sound of gentle breathing and Lynn snoring. Both girls were asleep.

"Zey can't see me," said PJ. "Or hear us. It iz only a dream."

"But how are you here now in reality as well as then in my dream?"

"To make sure you understood vot you saw, Leonora."

"I don't think I understand *anything* any more," I said. It was all so extraordinary. However, I couldn't deny that I felt better for having told someone what had happened with Poppy, even if PJ was a figment of my imagination.

"I can see vhy you feel so bad about your sister's death," he said, "but zere was nozing you could have done. It vas her time. If she hadn't gone zat way, she vould have gone another. Zere vas nozing you could do. You must understand zat. But here…" he indicated the sleeping shapes of Lynn and Marilyn, "here zere's a lot you can do."

"What do you mean?"

"Zink about it. Remember vat you've dreamt tonight. You'll find a vay. You vill, for in your heart, you're not a bad girl, Leonora Hedley-Dent."

And when he said that I felt like crying again.

Chapter Fourteen

Christmas Wishes

"And a Merry Christmas to you," groaned Lynn when the lights blasted on.

I leapt out of bed. "And a *Merry* Christmas to you," I said and I meant it. I felt totally, absolutely, amazingly brilliant.

Lynn and Marilyn both threw their pillows at me. "Shurrup will you?" they moaned in unison.

I felt like dancing, so I did. An Irish jig at the end of the bed.

"Come on," I said to the girls as the door opened and Mark poked his head around. "Get up. It's Christmas Day."

"But you don't do Christmas, remember?" said Marilyn.

Mark came in and sat on the end of Lynn's bed and he was soon joined by Jake. "Yeah. Are you on *drugs*, Leonora?" he asked.

I felt so good I hugged myself. "Nope. Just high on... life! God, it's good to be alive!" I stood on my head.

Just for the heck of it. When I saw the others' faces, I burst out laughing. Jake, Mark, Marilyn and Lynn were sitting up gawping at me with open mouths.

"Aliens have been in the night and eaten your brain, haven't they?" asked Jake.

"Jake. Jakey baby. Jake my man. My mate," I said then did a cartwheel down the middle of the aisle between beds, landed neatly at the end of Lynn's and gave him a hug. "Happy Chrimbole."

He pushed me off. "Wergh. Gerroff. You're *frightening* me!"

I went over and hugged Mark. He pushed me off too. "Cut the vomit stuff, Brat Princess. I don't buy it. What's the game? Is this some new trick to get out of here? Jake's already done the mad act. It didn't work. No point in you trying it, too... although I have to say that you're a lot more convincing than Jake was."

"Do you think we should ask Mario to get a doctor?" asked Marilyn. "I really think she might 'ave flipped."

I laughed again. "No. Not really. This is the season to be jolly and I am. Jolly that is. I feel good, no, not good, GREAT!" I began to sing. "Oh... jingle bells, jingle bells, jingle all the waaaaaaaay."

Lynn noticed a small pile of parcels by the door. "Hey look! Presents! Maybe they're for us!" She raced over to look and, indeed, the names on the labels were ours. "Hurray. Presents. I *love* presents."

There were two for me and one for everyone else. I quickly unwrapped my first one to find that it was a phone similar to the phone I'd destroyed on the first day I'd arrived. Gold with a large diamond on it. It was actually cute and I resolved that I wouldn't break it this time. In the second parcel was the necklace with the lion's head on it. I'd wondered where that had got to. Mr O must have found it and kept it for me.

In the meantime, the others had unwrapped their parcels too. Marilyn got a mug with Taurus written on it (that was her birth sign). Lynn got a pink baseball cap with a ram on it (she was an Aries) and a bottle of what looked like paint remover. She laughed then rolled up a sleeve and pointed at her tattoo. "It's not real. It's one of the ones that come off with the right remover. I got it done down the market. I don't even like tattoos."

"So why did you put it on?" I asked.

"To make me look hard but... I guess I don't need to do that any more."

I went and gave her a hug. "No you don't. We're all friends here."

"You're weird," she said. "What do you want?"

"Nothing," I replied. "To be friends. That's all."

She looked at me suspiciously, but I grinned back at her.

Mark got a tiny laptop and some computer games and a note saying, *For the next time you get bored.*

He looked well pleased with his gift.

"What did you get, Jake?" asked Lynn.

"Same as Mark. A dinky laptop and a computer game. A *car* computer game and there's a note with it. *It's safer to joyride these cars than real ones.* Hmm. I guess. What did you get Leonora?"

I showed them my phone and the necklace and the girls oohed and aahed. *Just imagine if they saw my collection back home,* I thought. One of my mobiles was made from real diamonds.

Mr O appeared at the door. "So did you give each other any gifts?" he asked.

Jake snorted. "What? Like a mouldy sock?"

"Or a potato?" asked Lynn. "We haven't got anything to give or hadn't you noticed?"

"Leonora..." said Mr O, and he gave me the same pointed look that he had given me the previous night at the camp fire.

"What?" I asked. "What am I supposed to give?" I put my hand up to my neck. "Not my locket. That's the only thing I've got here."

"No-one wants your poxy locket," sneered Marilyn.

Mr O sighed. "Your dreams, Leonora. Your encounter with Neptune and Pluto. Didn't you learn *anything* from them?"

"I... I..." I'd been so glad to wake up and realize that my dreams had been just dreams that I hadn't given them any further thought, but Mr O was staring at me like I'd missed something.

"Take five minutes all of you," he said and began to hand out paper and pens. "I thought each of you might like to send your parents a message seeing as it's Christmas Day. If you write to them, Hermie will be sure they get them some time today." With another pointed look in my direction, he left us alone.

I sat on the end of my bed, went through my dreams in my mind and racked my brain as to what it was that Mr O thought that I could do. As the dreams came back to me, the penny began to drop and I began to write my letter.

Dear Mummy and Daddy,

I am so sorry for all the trouble I have caused in the past years. I should have been better, I know I should. Poppy was your daughter as well as my sister and of course you miss her as much as I do. I am sorry I have been so selfish. It was my only way of coping and I cut myself off from you. Can you forgive me for being such a frightful pain?

I have one more week here and I don't mind a bit. I really don't. I have more to learn here and a lot more to do.

I do love you and I promise that when I come home, I will be a good girl. The old Leonora. I'm not the girl you sent here. I will change.

With lots of love and kisses,
Your daughter, Leo
XXX

After ten minutes, Mr O came back into the room and began to collect our letters. I glanced over at him and he gave me a nod.

"Ready, Leonora?" he asked.

I took a deep breath and nodded back to him. I knew what I had to do. "Okay everyone. Mr O was right before. I do have some gifts I'd like to give you. First for you, Jake. Happy Christmas. I'd like to pay for your little brother to get the best treatment that he needs, that is if you'll let me."

Jake's face crumpled. "Don't poke fun, Leonora," he said. "It's not funny."

"I'm not. *Really* I'm not, Jake. I have money. Lots of it. *Loads* of it. I don't need it all and, well... my little sister was ill once and... and I... I lost her. There was nothing I could do. But I *can* help you, that is if you'll let me."

Jake looked around at the others as if trying to work out what was happening but they looked equally as mystified as he did.

"You mean it?" Jake asked.

"I do. You have my solemn vow. Cross my heart and hope to die. I really mean it."

Jake took a long look at me as if trying to gauge if

I was messing with him then he thumped his forehead with the palm of his hand. "Oh I get it. You mean you'll *lend* it to me and you want interest?"

"*No*. NO! Honestly. No interest. This is a no-strings attached gift. Please. It would mean a lot to me." I felt horrified at his reaction and his lack of trust in me.

Jake looked right at me. "Why?"

"I want to help and... I want to be friends."

"Money can't buy you everything you know," said Jake. "Especially friends."

"Yes, of course. You're right. I'm so sorry. Okay. Forget the money. Sorry. I didn't mean to be offensive. I really didn't, but... I genuinely would like you to be my friend. It would mean a lot to me."

Jake nodded slowly. "Okay. Seeing as it's Christmas and even though you are a total stroppy cow, you are also quite a laugh. I will be your friend."

Marilyn rolled her eyes. "Oh for heaven's sake, Jake," she said, "take the dosh as well. Your family needs it and we can all see that she's on the level for once in her life."

"I am, but it's your choice, Jake," I said. "The money's still on the table if you want it."

The room fell silent as Jake considered the offer. After a few moments, he took a deep breath, coughed, then nodded. "Okay then. Deffo. Deal."

"Deal," I said.

Mr O beamed happily around the room. "Okay. So who's next?"

"You can give me a pile of dosh if you want," said Mark. "I ain't proud."

I remembered his family in my dream last night. The worried expressions of his parents. "How about I give you something else instead of dosh?"

"No. Money will be fine. And I'll be your friend, too, if you like."

"How about instead of money, I buy your family a house."

Mark sighed and looked sad. "Okay, so now I know that you're taking the mick. A doll's house, right? You're having a laugh, aren't you?"

I turned to Mr O. "Tell him, tell him I mean it."

Mr O nodded. "She's serious."

"I am," I said. "Look. I know I've been a pain since I got here and acted like a brat princess, but… well, a few things have become clear to me – like what matters. Family is one thing. Having a home another. And friends, too. So Mark, I'd like to help if you'll let me. As one friend to another. I'd like to buy your family a house. A real one. Okay, not a mansion, but a house. A home from where you can't be evicted." Mark's expression looked so hopeful that I knew I could never let him down. "I *really* mean it, don't I, Mr O? Tell him."

Mr O nodded. "She does. And she can. And I think she will."

Mark fell back onto his bed with a huge silly grin. "Mum and Dad are going to be so... wow! This is *amazing*. Like winning the lottery. The best Christmas present ever."

Lynn sidled up to me. "What about me?" she asked, then she sighed. "I don't need a house. Or medical help. What you gonna give me, princess?"

I already knew what I'd like to give Lynn. I'd decided days ago. Long before the dreams and my encounters with Saturn, Neptune and Pluto. I knew that I wanted to give her some kind of present because of all of them, in her own weird way, she had befriended me the most. "Don't you remember what you wanted?" I asked.

She shook her head.

"But you *told* me what you want Lynn. Friends. A pet. Pets are the best friends as they never judge and never let you down. Remember, I told you about my dog, Coco? I suggest that we go next week and get whatever you like. A rabbit, a dog, a cat, a goldfish. Whatever you want."

Lynn sniffed and pulled an "I'm not impressed" face. "Yeah. Okay. Cool. Yeah. Maybe a pit bull. Or a piranha – you know those fish that eat flesh or... a man-eating spider or a boa constrictor. What do you reckon?"

I must have looked shocked. I hadn't imagined that she'd want *killer* pets, but then she grinned. "Just messin' with ya, Leo. No. A couple of cutie-pie kittens would be fab."

"And what about Marilyn?" asked Mr O.

"I don't want anything," pouted Marilyn. "I don't need anything from 'er."

"Oh cut the tough act, Marilyn," I said. "I wouldn't leave you out and… although we haven't been the best of friends, we have been through a lot in here together. Please let me give you something too."

"I don't know if I want to be friends. You can't buy me as easily as the others."

"I'm not trying to buy you! I am trying to be NICE for a change…" I could feel a major strop coming on. *For heaven's sake*, I thought, *I try to do the decent things and boy, are they making it hard work!* I turned to Mr O and looked at him pleadingly. "I am *trying* to be good here and all I am getting back is *ingratitude* and *suspicion!*"

Mr O coughed. "Now then, Leonora, you haven't exactly been Princess Perfect since you got here. Can you blame them for being suspicious of your motives?"

I looked around at the group and had to admit, I hadn't exactly shown my *best* side. "Okay. Sorry. Sorry. You don't have to be my friend, Marilyn, not if you don't want to. Just, I thought that I could give you a shopping spree. The shopping spree that I was going to go on before I came here. In fact, I'll come with you if you like. It's always more fun if you go with a mate… not that you have to be my mate… no, I mean, it's more fun to go with someone. Oh never mind. Look. I know all the best boutiques in Paris and I don't really need any more clothes, so you can have my allowance as well. I have enough stuff. Well, okay, almost enough. Maybe I *could* do with a couple of pairs of shoes and a handbag and a… Actually… maybe I need a whole new wardrobe seeing as I am about a million times thinner now than when I came in here. Yeah, come to think of it, I need *loads* of things. Yeah. I ought to come with you."

Mr O and the boys cracked up laughing and for a second, I saw myself through their eyes.

"Oops! I'm doing the me-me-me thing again, aren't I? Sorry. Old habits blah de blah. Anyway. Shopping. You. Me. Gay Paree. Are you up for it. Marilyn?"

Marilyn shrugged. "Yeah maybe," she said. "If you play your cards right and don't go back to being the brat princess. I'll come with you if you be yourself. The real Leonora. You don't have to pretend to be some sister of mercy all of a sudden. I don't buy it."

"Okay," I agreed.

"And can I say something to you seeing as we're on about fashion?" Marilyn continued.

I nodded.

"You look so much better with your hair curly. It suits

your personality to be wild down your back. It's like a manifestation of your character."

"Yeah. And your eyes look better brown," added Lynn. "Better with your colouring."

"Yeah," chorused Jake and Mark.

"Huh," I said, and I rolled my eyes up to the ceiling. "Like I'm going to listen to a bunch of losers like you for fashion advice."

For a moment their faces dropped.

"Only joshing," I said. Actually I was pleased with my new look. I could see for myself that I looked a lot better. I was fitter, too. The spots had gone. And it was a relief not to have to spend hours straightening my hair every morning.

"You know what, Princess?" said Lynn. "You're all right. You're going to fit in after all. In't she, Marilyn?"

Marilyn nodded. "Yeah. And... well... we have something to say to you too. We woz pulling your leg weren't we? About being murderers and all."

I creased up laughing. "I knew that. You're not tough enough by half."

"You neither,' smiled Marilyn. "You know, I guess we're not that different after all. We both put on an act. And we both have parents who are under some mad presumption that being here might make us nicer people."

"As if," said Lynn.

"Yeah," said Marilyn. She looked awkward for a moment. "I was teased about my background at my last school – that's why I put on the tough accent here, so that no-one would make fun of me."

"No need," I said. "We won't bully you here."

"No way," said Mark.

"Now what about you Leonora?" asked Mr O. "Is there anything that you want?"

"Er… could I possibly have my credit cards back?"

Mr O nodded. "I think that can be arranged, but I think I know what you have in mind and you might not need them as Jupiter is…"

"You going to organize a private plane out of here?" Jake interrupted.

I shook my head. "No. Not just yet because… if I'm allowed, I'd like to help make Christmas. Right here. If you'll let me…" I glanced over at Mr O and he nodded. "Okay, we're going to have the best Christmas breakfast and lunch ever. And roaring fires in all the grates. And games. And presents. And chocolates. And…"

Lynn shrieked. "And *snow!*"

I nodded. "Well that would be nice, but I'm not sure that you can get snow with an American Express card…"

Lynn pointed up at the window. She was right. It had started to snow. I raced to the window and saw that the sky was heavy with black clouds, and white flakes had begun to fall, coating the lawn and the trees and shrubs outside. It looked so magical as the rising sun caught the flakes and made them sparkle with a million tiny stars.

"And ya-hey," cried Jake. "Joe's back!"

"As I was trying to tell you, you won't have to wait long for that Christmas breakfast," said Mr O.

There outside the kitchen door was the man from the deli. Joe. He was dressed up as Santa and he was unloading the best breakfast feast I had ever seen. He saw us watching him, gave us a cheery wave and beckoned us to go to the kitchen.

The others made a dash for it, but I held back for a few moments.

"Not joining the others?" asked Mr O.

"In a sec," I said. "I just wanted to say thank you whoever you are, a planet, a guardian or whatever. You've been great and, even in this dismal place, it's clear that you're a real star."

Mr O flushed pink with pleasure. "You too, Leonora. You too." Then he cleared his throat and offered me his arm. "Now let's go eat and get warm. And not before time, I say, because, you think this place has been an ordeal for you? Hah! I can tell you now, dingy, cold places are *not* my scene at all. So let's go light a few fires, get that feast organized and have ourselves a proper merry Christmas."

"Sounds like a top plan," I said with a grin as I took his arm.

Epilogue

I got to go home on New Year's Day. Mummy and Daddy were in the hall at the lodge just after breakfast and had a helicopter waiting in the grounds outside to whisk me away. It was wonderful to see their kind, familiar faces once again.

Before we returned to the Caribbean, I went to a store and bought an angel's outfit, complete with white feather wings and a halo (not for me, I wasn't that deluded!). I gave it to Shirla when I got home to give to her granddaughter so that she could be a Christmas angel after all. It was my way of saying sorry for being an almighty pain for so long and I think Shirla was really touched.

My new pal, Mr O came to visit us in the Caribbean. He said he likes the climate better there and, while he was with us, he confessed that I was one of his favourite Zodiacs Girls because I was his biggest challenge. I never did get whether the zodiac thing was legit or whether he was actually certifiable and, with the rest of his strange mates, a candidate for la-la land. He never mentioned it again after my month as Zodiac Girl and neither did I. Whatever. In the end, it didn't matter. We got a result and that's what counts. One of the unexpected bonuses from my time in the boot camp was that I looked a whole lot better. Everyone commented. No spots or flab. And I've stayed as slim as I was in the lodge. Okay, so I'm not a size zero, but I don't want to be any more. I want to feel good and be healthy. I came out of the boot camp feeling fab and put it down to the simple fresh food we had in there and plenty of exercise. Shirla, Coco and I go jogging down on the beach most days now (although in Shirla's case it's more like wobbling), and Mason's learned to cook delicious meals that aren't fattening. He can even make porridge taste divine with fresh fruits. (There was no way I was going to carry on eating it the way they served it at the lodge. I don't believe in suffering beyond the call of duty.)

I stayed in touch with my boot-camp inmates and count them among my closest friends although we live in different countries (Mummy and Daddy got me into a local school so I don't have to board and be away from them any more). All of them email regularly and we speak on the phone when we can. Marilyn and

Lynn went back to their school and were elected to run the school bookshop, with great success apart from the nights they sneak in the crème de menthe liqueur and have to be carried home singing rugby songs. Mark decided that he wanted to be an actor, specializing in mime. I think that he'll be good at it and, from his emails, it sounds like he is happy now that he knows what he wants to do with his life and has a secure home. Sadly, although Jake's brother went on to make a terrific recovery, Jake never did get over his addiction to joyriding. After nicking a silver Merc, he got caught driving the wrong way down the motorway singing God Save the Queen with his boxers on his head at four in the morning. Luckily he didn't hit anyone or anything but he was locked up for two years. *C'est la vie.* You can't win them all.

And in case you're wondering if I let Shirla, Mason or Henry off their debt? No way! Excuse me, do I look sucker of the year? But I *did* let them off the interest. I'm not a total Scrooge. They earn a stonkload of dosh compared to other people so give me a break, I'm not the *only* person who had lessons to learn. Like, reality check – they shouldn't have been borrowing money from a *fourteen* year-old head case who didn't know any better!

The best news though, was that, the year after my time in the boot camp, I was on the front cover of *Teen*

Vogue and there was an article about me inside saying "I was the teenager who best knew how to keep Christmas well." A fact I pride myself on actually. Oh yes. I am Queen of Generosity, I really am. Even though I say so myself. Oh yes. Ding dong merrily on wotsit. Bring it on and deck the halls with Christmas holly, yada yada yada. I'll be there. Every year in December. Okay, so maybe on a yacht somewhere fabbie dabbie doobie. But why not? I can afford it and hey – *'tis* the season to be jolly.

So, indeed. Peace on Earth and God bless us. Every one.

The Leo Files

Characteristics, Facts and Fun

July 23 – August 23

Loyal and proud, Leos are vibrant and larger than life. Leos love to be noticed and admired. They will do anything to gain your attention. This sign is creative, and they will push themselves until they reach the top of whatever ladder they happen to be climbing!

Although there's always something interesting going on around a Leo, don't forget to duck when they don't get their own way. These guys can be arrogant, proud, pushy and haughty. They like to receive compliments, so if you haven't given them one for a while expect to get some of the famous fiery Leo temper!

Element:	Fire
Colour:	Gold, orange
Birthstone:	Ruby, diamond
Animal:	Dog
Lucky day:	Sunday
Planet:	Ruled by the Sun

A Leo's best friends are likely to be:
Aries
Sagittarius
Libra

A Leo's enemies are likely to be:
Virgo
Scorpio

A Leo's idea of heaven would be:
If it was their birthday every day – constant attention and compliments!

A Leo would go mad if:
They were set tasks to clean, cook and wait on other people.

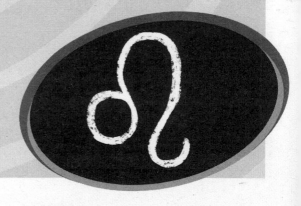

Celebrity Leos

July 23	✳	**Woody Harrelson**
July 24	✳	**Jennifer Lopez**
July 25	✳	**Matt LeBlanc**
July 26	✳	**Mick Jagger**
July 28	✳	**Beatrix Potter**
July 30	✳	**Arnold Schwarzenegger**
July 31	✳	**J. K. Rowling**
August 1	✳	**Yves Saint Laurent**
August 2	✳	**Wes Craven**
August 5	✳	**Neil Armstrong**
August 6	✳	**Geri Halliwell**
August 7	✳	**Charlize Theron**

August 8	✳	**Dustin Hoffman**
August 9	✳	**Whitney Houston**
August 10	✳	**Antonio Banderas**
August 11	✳	**Hulk Hogan**
August 12	✳	**Pete Sampras**
August 13	✳	**Alfred Hitchcock**
August 14	✳	**Halle Berry**
August 15	✳	**Ben Affleck**
August 16	✳	**Madonna**
August 17	✳	**Robert De Niro**
August 18	✳	**Patrick Swayze**
August 19	✳	**Matthew Perry**
August 21	✳	**Kim Cattrall**

Leonora's DIY Spa Facial

There's nothing better than pampering yourself with a fabulous face pack, and you can find all the ingredients for this luxurious treat at home or in the garden!

Rich rose and honey mask

You will need:

6 fresh rose petals

2 tbsps rose water

1 tbsp natural yogurt, room temperature (not low fat or non-fat)

1 tbsp runny honey (to make honey runny, you can warm it in a microwave for a few seconds).

Preparation:

Soak the rose petals in water, then crush them in a bowl. Add the rosewater, yogurt and honey. Mix well and apply the mixture to your face – don't get it in your eyes! Leave on for 10 minutes while you do your nails ... Rinse the gooey mess off your face with warm water and wait for the compliments to start!

Are you a typical Leo?

Your bossy teacher tells you to get involved in more after-school activities. What do you choose?

A) The photography club – hours in the darkroom by yourself, what could be better?

B) The school choir – so you can work as part of a team.

C) Student president. You'd be by far the best candidate.

Your friend has a date and needs advice on what to wear. She asks to borrow something of yours – what do you say?

A) No way! Your clothes are way too nice to lend out. You offer to go shopping with her instead.

B) I suppose so . . . you make sure she knows that if she ruins it, she replaces it!

C) Absolutely! Your wardrobe is way cooler than hers and you don't mind lending.

It's the school holidays. What do you do with your days?

A) Nothing. Lazing around is what holidays are for!

B) Trips to the cinema, reading books – nothing too energetic.

C) As much as you can fit in! Swimming, frisbee at the park, parties and dance classes – the possibilities are endless!

Look into the future . . . what's your ideal job?

A) Something that makes a difference – maybe working for a charity.

B) You don't mind, as long as you make loads of money!

C) An actress or a singer – something that will make you super-famous!

You're going to the school prom and you need a date. Who do you ask?

A) Your next-door neighbour – you've known him forever and he'll do.

B) The best-looking guy at school – he's bound to say yes.

C) No one – you're sure that someone will ask you first.

You're desperate to go to a party but you're grounded. How do you persuade your parents to let you go?

A) Be reasonable and tell them why you would like

to go. You're sure they'll understand.

B) Turn on the waterworks. A few tears and they'll be putty in your hands.

C) Shout and scream and stamp your feet. They'll say yes to get you to shut up!

How did you score?

Mostly As – lacklustre Leo
Are you sure you're a Leo? Quiet, reasonable and shy aren't in most Leo's vocabularies . . .

Mostly Bs – lovely Leo
It sounds like your Leo side is being influenced by another sign, but it's still pretty strong.

Mostly Cs – loudmouth Leo
ROAR! You're Leo through and through.

From Geek to Goddess

Cathy Hopkins

This time it's a Gemini!

An outgoing Gemini, Gemma is stuck at boarding school with a boring mousy room-mate and a bully who's out to get her. Things look bleak until she's chosen as a Zodiac Girl. Can Gemma make the right choices to find new friends?

Bridesmaids' Club

Cathy Hopkins

This time it's a Libra!

Planning her big sister's dream wedding is the perfect job for Libran Chloe – until the planets choose her to be a Zodiac Girl and the dream ceremony turns into her worst nightmare. Can bridesmaid Chloe save the big day?

A selected list of titles available from Kingfisher, an imprint of Macmillan Children's Books

The prices shown below are correct at the time of going to press. However, Macmillan Publishers reserves the right to show new retail prices on covers, which may differ from those previously advertised.

Cathy Hopkins

Zodiac Girls: Dancing Queen	978-0-7534-1765-2	£5.99
Zodiac Girls: Discount Diva	978-0-7534-1503-0	£5.99
Zodiac Girls: From Geek to Goddess	978-0-330-51029-5	£5.99
Zodiac Girls: Brat Princess	978-0-330-51028-8	£5.99
Zodiac Girls: Star Child	978-0-330-51032-5	£5.99
Zodiac Girls: The Bridesmaids' Club	978-0-330-51027-1	£5.99
Zodiac Girls: Double Trouble	978-0-330-51020-2	£5.99
Zodiac Girls: Recipe for Rebellion	978-0-330-51025-7	£5.99

All Pan Macmillan titles can be ordered from our website, www.panmacmillan.com, or from your local bookshop and are also available by post from:

Bookpost, PO Box 29, Douglas, Isle of Man IM99 1BQ
Credit cards accepted. For details:
Telephone: 01624 677237
Fax: 01624 670 923
Email: bookshop@enterprise.net
www.bookpost.co.uk

Free postage and packing in the United Kingdom